PUFFIN BOOKS

Editor: Kaye Webb

THE WORKHOUSE CHILD

'I do love trains!' said Pansy.

'Delicious, aren't they?' said her friend Atalanta's grandmother.

Atalanta herself didn't say anything.

Halfway to the seaside they changed trains, and while they waited they put pennies in a slot-machine to have their fortunes told. Atalanta's card said she was going to come into money, her grandmother's was about a dark handsome visitor, but Pansy's was different – more mysterious and baffling, and really rather frightening for someone who wasn't used to paying visits on her own.

What Pansy's fortune said was: 'Do not be dismayed if you find yourself among strangers. Rely on your own resources and you will contrive to extricate yourself with a certain amount of difficulty.' What did it mean? What strangers? She didn't want to be among them!

'Do not be dismayed,' said Atalanta's grandmother comfortingly, but sure enough Pansy was soon on the run, terrified and hungry, dressed in a poor workhouse girl's clothes, alone in a horrible world where people chased and hunted her to hand her over to the cruel workhouse master and matron. And she had nothing to show who she was and where she really belonged . . .

This fast-moving story, frightening and funny by turns, will appeal to girls of ten and over.

Cover design by Alexy Pendle

GERALDINE SYMONS

The Workhouse Child

ILLUSTRATED BY ALEXY PENDLE

PUFFIN BOOKS

Puffin Books, Penguin Books Ltd, Harmondsworth, Middlesex, England
Penguin Books, 625 Madison Avenue, New York, New York 10022, U.S.A.
Penguin Books Australia Ltd, Ringwood, Victoria, Australia
Penguin Books Canada Ltd, 2801 John Street, Markham, Ontario, Canada L3R 1B4
Penguin Books (N.Z.) Ltd, 182–190 Wairau Road, Auckland 10, New Zealand

—

First published by Macmillan & Co Ltd 1969
Published in Puffin Books 1972
Reprinted 1976, 1977

—

Copyright © Geraldine Symons, 1969
Illustrations copyright © Macmillan & Co. Ltd, 1969

—

Made and printed in Great Britain
by Richard Clay (The Chaucer Press), Ltd,
Bungay, Suffolk
Set in Linotype Georgian

To Claire for herself

CONTENTS

1

A JOURNEY AND FORTUNES

THAT evening Nana laid out Pansy's clothes to be packed on Pansy's bed. Her bathing-dress and cap and folded water-wings looked almost as exciting and out of place in the middle of the counterpane as a bit of seaweed or a crab.

'Although you're only going for less than a fortnight –' Nana said.

'Ten whole days,' Pansy interrupted her, 'not counting tomorrow, Tuesday, when we go, and Saturday week when we come back.'

'Although you're only going for ten whole days,' Nana began again, I'm sending you with three lots of under-clothes in case you have an accident.'

'What sort of an accident?'

'I don't know and I hope you won't have one, but you're so scatter-brained sometimes you might do something silly like falling down in the sea, though goodness knows you're old enough now to be sensible. And don't forget to clean your nails, mind. I'm putting this orange-stick in your sponge-bag and you're to clean them every day without fail.'

'I don't think,' said Pansy slowly, 'that Atalanta's grand-mother would notice if they weren't clean.'

'It doesn't matter a mite whether she does or not; you're still to clean them.'

'Nobody ever seems to mind what Atalanta does,' Pansy pursued. 'Her grandmother never seems to *tell* her to do anything, and her parents don't mind a fig, Atalanta says. It must be funny to have parents who are so busy being famous. Atalanta says if she ran away in the holidays they wouldn't have time to look for her.'

'Well, I hope she won't do anything so stupid,' Nana laid two clean folded white cotton nighties on the bed, 'and I've yet to see Atalanta run.'

Pansy giggled. 'She never does; she won't.'

'She won't do a lot of things it seems, and as for all that talk of hers about her parents,' Nana pursed her lips, 'I'll judge whether it's twaddle or not when I see them.'

'But they never come here, so how can you? They never come to see Atalanta.' Pansy did wish they would. She wanted to see them most frightfully herself, but although Atalanta lived with her grandmother at Winsbury in the term-time, her parents never came for a special occasion, or simply to see how she was getting on, as the boarders' parents sometimes did, and Atalanta had been at school a whole year now.

'You'd have thought Mr Robertson-Fortescue would come to see his mother sometimes,' Nana said, but she knew the answer already. Pansy, to whom the same thought had often occurred, had thrashed out the whole question with Atalanta, and told Nana all about it. 'He doesn't come to see me,' Atalanta had explained, 'because he sees enough of me in the holidays.'

'But you said he just wrote, shut up in his room,' Pansy had protested.

'He has to come out to eat and then if I'm eating he sees me,' Atalanta had replied, as though it was idiotic of Pansy not to realize.

'But your grandmother's his mother; doesn't he ever want to see her?'

'He sees her when she comes up.'

Up was London. Atalanta went up to London, to her home, at the end of the term, or had till now. These holidays were going to be different. She wasn't going straight back to London. Her grandmother was taking her to the sea and had invited Pansy to go with them.

When Nana had gone to the nursery to sew a button on one of Pansy's shoes and had left Pansy to search in her dressing-table drawer for her second hair-ribbon, Aunt Katie came into the bedroom. Looking at the collection on the bed, she said, 'You are not to bathe without your wings, Pansy.'

'But I can swim! I did for a minute when we went to the sea last year, really I did.'

'A minute isn't enough. It's no good saying you won't go out of your depth; you may go without meaning to. That coast has a way of shelving – one minute you're up to your waist, and the next you're up to your chin, and Lavinia Robertson-Fortescue isn't likely to notice. Not if she's painting,' Aunt Katie added, rather as though she were talking to herself.

'Can she only think of one thing at a time?' Pansy asked. 'That's what Grandfather said was having a one track mind.'

'Lavinia's mind is excessively versatile,' Aunt Katie said.

'Versatile?' Pansy wasn't sure what *versatile* meant.

'Yes, it goes from one thing to another with the greatest of ease – though it might not go to the fact that you were drowning if she was deep in her painting,' Aunt Katie explained. 'Lavinia is very original. She takes after her mother. I never met her mother, but I once saw a painting of her. It was when Papa – your great-grandfather – took Aunt Susu and me when we were children to the Exhibition at the Royal Academy. There was a picture, a very large one – I can see it now,' said Aunt Katie reflectively, 'although I've never seen it since – of the three lovely Chatty sisters. Cordelia, Lavinia's mother, was the eldest. They were all three in white robes and one was holding a harp. I think they were meant to look like angels.'

'Did they?' asked Pansy delightedly.

'I dare say they did to some people, but Aunt Susu and I thought they looked rather silly – but then we were only children.'

'Did they have haloes?'

'Not that I remember. A few years later, Cordelia had a severe illness and after that she retired into her shell and wrote poetry. I read some of her poems once and I came to the conclusion' – Aunt Katie went over to the window and stood looking out – 'that she must have been rather a weird creature.'

Pansy tried to see the vision with her mind's eye, the vision of a weird creature in a white robe crawling into a shell. She saw a conch shell, with a pink inside, one of those big shells that make a noise like the sea when you hold them to your ear. She could see the shell quite plainly, but it was very difficult to see Atalanta's grandmother's lovely mother doing something so extraordinary. While Pansy was still trying to see it, Aunt Katie went on in a musing voice rather as though she were talking to herself, 'Lavinia must have had a strange upbringing. I remember her telling us once, at a tea-party, that she had had a governess for two years, and when she left she had never had another.'

'Didn't she go to school?' asked Pansy.

'No, apparently not, but she must have read a great deal. She is most cultured, and I admire her for than.' Aunt Katie sounded a little bit as if she didn't admire her for absolutely everything. She didn't seem to really admire her for going to Paris. 'Lavinia insisted on going to Paris to learn painting when she was sixteen. How her parents could have let her...'

'Perhaps she ran away –' Pansy suggested eagerly.

No, Aunt Katie didn't think she had. Then she changed the subject, which was disappointing; Pansy would much rather have heard more about Atalanta's grandmother. Turning away from the window, Aunt Katie came back towards the bed. 'You must try to be helpful while you're away.'

'How?' Pansy screwed round her nose which had suddenly started to tickle. 'What shall I do?'

'It depends – you will have to wait and see. I have no doubt there will be things you can do – little politenesses like carrying baskets on picnics, things of that kind.'

'They can be my good deeds!'

Aunt Katie already knew what Miss Lamb had said at prayers yesterday: 'I want each one of you to do one good deed every day throughout the holidays.' Eight weeks and two days of good deeds; Pansy had worked it out with the calendar. This morning there had been fifty-eight deeds waiting to be done. There were fifty-seven now, since she had done up Grandfather's bootlace.

Aunt Katie took Pansy to the station; they went in the cab. The train went at 2.48. Atalanta and her grandmother hadn't arrived by the ticket office and they weren't on Platform Three when Aunt Katie and Pansy arrived there. 'I hope they won't miss the train,' said Aunt Katie, 'there isn't another today.'

'Whatever shall we do if they do?' cried Pansy frantically.

'Go home and try again tomorrow. It would be an anticlimax I'm afraid, but life is made up of them.'

'Would I unpack?' asked Pansy, appalled.

'Not everything – just the things you wanted for the night, like your brush and comb, but it won't be necessary: here they are!'

Pansy gasped with relief, 'Where?' Then she saw them across the railway line on Platform Two from which they would have to go down the subway to get to Platform Three. Atalanta's grandmother had on a green dress and something blue round her neck, and a large floppy hat crowded with flowers. Even from this distance Pansy could well see it was a glorious thing. Grandfather always called Mrs Robertson-Fortescue's clothes her 'plumage'. Pansy was looking forward to staring at her; she always liked to and now there were seven days of staring ahead of her, and, after the things that Aunt Katie had told her, Atalanta's grandmother seemed more interesting than ever. 'You mustn't mention anything I said, of course. I was just *ruminating*,' Aunt Katie had explained.

Now Aunt Katie said, 'We'll just wave; we don't want to shout across the line.'

Mrs Robertson-Fortescue had no such qualms. 'Here we are,' she called in her vague trailing kind of voice which carried very well all the same.

There were four other people waiting on the platform which made Pansy too embarrassed to shout back, quite apart from what Aunt Katie had said. She grinned instead.

13

Atalanta did nothing. She thought waving silly, and never smiled when she was supposed to.

Aunt Katie changed her mind and called back quietly, 'We've only just come.'

When Atalanta and her grandmother had disappeared down the subway in the wake of the porter with their luggage, Aunt Katie said that no one but an artist would have worn such a strange collection of colours – grass green and sky-blue and that hat – but as Lavinia was an artist she supposed they must be all right. 'She always looks very distinguished in her own particular way.'

Pansy said, 'Wasn't her hat *lovely*!'

'Too lovely. If the wind takes it out to sea, don't you go after it.'

'Couldn't I with my wings?'

'No. You'd go on chasing it and before you could say "knife" you'd be out to sea.'

'I'm sure I could say "knife" first.'

'A hat's not worth drowning for – even *that* hat.'

'But what shall I say if she asks me to get it?'

'She won't, but if she does simply say I've told you not to swim out of your depth.'

Pansy glanced unhappily at the line. There was some orange peel on the other side. 'She'll think I'm afraid.'

'No, she won't; she'll understand perfectly I'm sure.'

Pansy wasn't sure at all, but while she was still thinking how awful it would be if she didn't understand, Mrs Robertson-Fortescue and Atalanta and the porter came up from the subway just as the train came in.

When Pansy had finished waving to Aunt Katie, and the train, which had been very slow in starting, had run out of the station, she flumped down in her corner seat. They all had corners; they had the carriage to themselves. Before she had another good look at Atalanta's grandmother, and she'd looked a good deal already, there was the town to be stared at. 'There's the cathedral! – and there's Shoemaker Row! Where's the school?'

'Where it's always been unfortunately. What on earth do

you want to stare at things you've been seeing for years for, as though you'd never seen them before?' said Atalanta. She was looking very untidy. Her pigtail was hairy-looking as though she'd gone to bed without undoing it and hadn't done it since, which was almost as awful as if she'd gone to bed in her clothes. She hadn't, Pansy decided. Her frock was not as crumpled as that – *quite*. It was brown, with pomegranates embroidered round the hem and neck and sleeves by her grandmother. Pansy had seen it before so she knew all about it. She had seen more of Mrs Robertson-Fortescue's plumage by now, too. There were all kinds of flowers on her hat – a glorious red rose, lilies of the valley, lilac, cowslips and a purple and white auricula. Atalanta had thrown her panama on the seat. It had nothing on it, no pomegranates, not even a ribbon. Pansy's was new with a white ribbon. In her clean green and white check frock with her hat on her head she felt inartistic and undistinguished. Snatching off her hat, she threw it down beside her.

'Happy, darling?' Mrs Robertson-Fortescue smiled at her.

Pansy, who wasn't used to being asked if she was happy only why she wasn't if she wasn't, said, yes, thank you, she was. But suppose she hadn't been, how could she have said 'No'?

'I do love trains!' It burst out of her.

'Delicious, aren't they?'

How could a train be delicious? That was the splendid thing about Atalanta's grandmother – the extraordinary words she used.

'I'd rather fly,' said Atalanta.

'*Fly?*' exclaimed Pansy, and then wished she hadn't, as though she didn't know about Monsieur Blériot who had flown from France to England right over the English Channel last summer.

'Like Monsieur Blériot in an aeroplane or like Daedalus and Icarus?' her grandmother inquired.

'Who were they?' Pansy asked.

'Daedalus was a mythological craftsman – a craftsman in Greek mythology, darling – who made wings for himself and his son, Icarus, and stuck them on to their shoulders with wax. Icarus flew too near the sun and the wax melted and he was killed.'

'How awful!' Pansy saw Icarus flapping up to the sun and the wax streaming down like the wax on a candle and the wings falling off and Icarus hurtling down head first, and then she saw Atalanta doing exactly the same. 'How awful if yours melted, Atalanta.'

'I wouldn't be so idiotic as to stick them on with wax and if I *was* such a fool I wouldn't go near the sun.'

No, she wouldn't, Pansy knew. Sitting there looking solid and sensible, not exactly dirty and not exactly clean, Atalanta did make it seem as though she wouldn't. 'What would you stick them on with?'

'Nothing. I should go by aeroplane of course.'

The train went into a tunnel. There was no light. In the noisy darkness which Pansy hated Atalanta shouted, 'I shall call you "Nonna".'

This surprising announcement steadied Pansy. 'Why?' she shrieked.

'Not you! It's the Italian for *grandmother*. It's more sophisticated than *Granny*.'

'Foreign words often seem to be,' her grandmother called back, 'and I dare say *Granny* might seem more so to the Italians than *Nonna*.'

'What shall I call you?' Pansy shouted. Everyone at home had agreed that Mrs Robertson-Fortescue was a tiring mouthful but that you couldn't call someone who wasn't your grandmother, 'Granny'.

'I expect the matter will dissolve itself,' Aunt Susu had said.

'*Nonna*', called Atalanta now.

'Yes, *Nonna*,' agreed her grandmother.

Even if it did mean grandmother it didn't sound like it, thought Pansy happily.

Just as the whole business was settled the train came out of the tunnel into daylight.

The journey was very slow; the train kept on stopping at country stations. After a door had slammed behind a departing passenger – or no one had departed, but something had been taken out or put in the guard's van – it seemed as though everyone had gone to sleep. 'Perhaps they're under a spell,' suggested Pansy. She was longing to get to their destination so frightfully she could hardly contain herself.

'I hope we won't go to sleep for fifty years. We should all feel very out-moded, I expect, when we woke up,' Nonna said. 'Instead of a skirt to my ankles I might find it ought to be up to my knees. How ridiculous!' She laughed gaily. 'Just fancy.'

Fancying, Pansy thought it so funny she laughed uproariously.

'I ought to wear trousers, I expect,' said Atalanta.

'In that case, it would be better if you went on sleeping,' said her grandmother with decision.

The station where they had to change was quite big and busy. They had three-quarters of an hour to wait. When they had had tea, and currant cakes that tasted of heavy baked suet, in the buffet, they put pennies in a slot-machine and had their fortunes told. The fortunes were printed on small cards.

Nonna's card said: *A dark handsome visitor is coming to see you from over the water. Do not rebuff him.*

'How deliciously mysterious. Naturally I shan't rebuff him unless he gives me good cause; he may be quite delightful, but if he isn't' – Nonna did up the button of her white kid glove – 'I shall most certainly get rid of him.'

Atalanta's fortune was quite different: *Your financial position is about to improve. Abstain from squandering your new-found riches and do not be too proud to accept advice from a friend.*

'What friend?' said Atalanta.

'Me!' said Pansy, 'It must be me, you haven't got another one here.'

'You don't know anything about money – you haven't even got to stocks and shares in arithmetic,' said Atalanta dampingly.

No, Pansy hadn't. She hadn't got the hang of vulgar fractions either.

'It doesn't necessarily mean this minute,' said Nonna.

'You may meet another friend later, in London, or it may not mean advice about money – in which case it might be Pansy who advises you. We must wait and see.'

'I've got more sense than she has.'

Yes, Atalanta had, Pansy knew, but she didn't mind. Agog with excitement, she put her penny in the slot and pulled out the little drawer with her fortune card in it. Snatching it eagerly, she read it aloud: *Do not be dismayed if you find yourself among strangers. Rely on your own resources and you will contrive to extricate yourself with a certain amount of difficulty.* What did it mean? What strangers? She didn't want to be among them! She would much rather have had Atalanta's fortune. 'I don't want to go among strangers!'

'Do not be dismayed,' said Nonna.

'You aren't strangers – it doesn't mean you, does it?'

'Of course not, dearest child, how could it?'

Looking up at Nonna's face, pale and lovely under her great flowered hat, Pansy felt a little rude. 'I only meant there weren't any other strangers.'

'Extricate yourself at once,' said Atalanta in her deep voice that began in her boots. 'If there was a train going the wrong way you could jump on that. There isn't, so you'll have the difficulty of burrowing through that hedge over there and lying flat on your face in a ditch. We are spies, Nonna and I, and we shoot to kill.' Atalanta was only joking of course, but her eyes had stopped blinking and glared at Pansy, without any laughter, through her spectacles.

Spies were often quite everyday kind of people whom none of their friends would suspect in their wildest dreams, Grandfather had said. He had told them about a mild musical little man who loved pottering in his garden. His name was George Smith and he had been selling information to the enemy for years. 'What happened to him?' Ginie had asked. 'He was executed,' said Grandfather. Bending double, he had cut through the stem of a marrow. 'Did he have his head cut off?' Pansy had asked and Grandfather had said, 'No, shot.'

She did hope that Atalanta and Nonna wouldn't turn out to be spies. She had the most dreadful vision of them being shot, standing side by side in front of a wall, Nonna in her flowery hat. But certainly they were not strangers.

2

DOWN TO THE SEA

PANSY had never stayed in a farmhouse before. It was a great change from the house in the Close, where the cathedral green was kept cut like a lawn and the elms grew straight out of it, neat and ordinary, without any bushes at their feet. Leaning out of the window of the bedroom she was to share with Atalanta, she felt mad with joy, it was all so wild and different. There was a dark red rose coming right up to the window. It was tangled and old-looking. Peering down into it, Pansy saw a nest only just below. If only she had been here when the eggs were there!

'If you had been,' Atalanta said, 'the bird would have deserted with you staring at it.'

There was a strip of grass and then a long jumbled flower bed in front of a low wall enclosing a yard with sheds on one side. There was some manure, and chickens scratching about, and an elder bush over the wall at the end.

'That's the midden,' said Atalanta. 'I bet there's some horse-flies on the manure. They bite like mad.'

'Perhaps,' Pansy dropped her voice, 'they won't know we're here!'

'They smell, silly.'

'How do you know? You don't live in the country; you live in London.'

'You don't have to live in a place to know about the things in it – and anyway I don't *live* in London; the terms are much longer than the holidays and now it's holidays I'm here.'

So dreadful not to be wanted at home. Sometimes when Pansy thought about Atalanta, when she wasn't there, her heart ached for her. So dreadful to have a mother who only lived for her acting, and a father who shut himself up all day in his study and wrote. But it hadn't ached so much since Aunt Katie had said to Nana, 'I shouldn't waste too much pity on Atalanta. She's a child who likes to dramatize herself. With parents like that it's hardly surprising.' Like what? Did Aunt Katie know something awful about them? Pansy's skin had begun to prickle a little with excitement. 'Like what?' she asked. 'A mother who acts and a father who writes; they both create drama,' Aunt Katie had explained. Although Pansy didn't want Atalanta's parents to be dreadful, exactly, she had felt a bit flat. 'Do you mean she pretends they don't want her when they do?' she had asked, shocked. 'Not having met them – only having seen her mother on the stage where she was extremely good,' Aunt Katie had said reminiscently, 'and never having met her father – I cannot tell you how much they want her, but I should not be in the least surprised to find that Atalanta was indulging in a bit of make-believe.' When Pansy had said why should she want to, that *she* wouldn't want to pretend her mother and father didn't want her, Aunt Katie had said, 'Of course you wouldn't, but you are not Atalanta.'

No, Pansy wasn't Atalanta. But now when she came to the business of the bed she wished she were. 'What side do you want?' she asked Atalanta.

'The one nearest the window.'

'So do I, but you have it – you're older, although I'm the guest. I want you to, it's my good deed for today.'

'No, you have it, then it can be my good deed for eleven nights,' said Atalanta.

Eleven good deeds – no need to do any more till they went home. How clever Atalanta was, thought Pansy, chagrined. 'I thought of it first.'

'You didn't think of eleven good deeds, you only thought of one, but all right, I'll have it and I'll have done my good deeds too by letting you do yours.' Bending, Atalanta wrenched off a garter and pulled down her stocking. Her leg was the colour of pastry with freckles on it.

Although Pansy was cross with her for having got every-

thing – the best side of the bed and eleven good deeds too –
she couldn't help saying, 'Can we take them off? In the
daytime?'

'Of course. I shan't put mine on again till I go home, if
then.'

Pansy stopped pulling at her garter and suddenly leapt
into the middle of the bed and turning on her back and
shooting her legs up into the air, sang 'Goodie, goodie,
goodie,' up and down the scale. Then, jumping off the bed,
she shouted, 'I shall put on my sand shoes!' When she had
unlocked her box with the key that Aunt Katie and Nana
had told her not to lose, and struggled with the clasps, she
flung open the lid and delved to the bottom. Her sand-shoes
were in the shoe-bag with rosebuds on it.

There was time to go to the beach before supper. There
was a track through the downs. Nonna set off still in her
flowery hat. There was no wind. 'I needn't refuse to save it,'
thought Pansy with relief. When she had begged to be
allowed to bathe, expecting to be told to wait till tomorrow,
Nonna had said, 'Why not?' Why not, indeed? But Nana
and the Aunts would have said it was too late.

There were lovely wild flowers on the downs, Nonna said.
Stooping, she picked a little pink one, 'Centaury,' she murmured, 'and hare-bells.'

Pansy loved wild flowers but she didn't want to stop now.
She couldn't think of anything but getting to the sea.
Atalanta didn't look as though she was thinking about the
sea at all. She was walking slowly along, staring in front of
her, reciting from the *Lays of Ancient Rome*. Her bathing
bundle had come undone and the towel was trailing on the
ground. '*O, Tiber! Father Tiber!*'

'Your towel's trailing. Do come on,' Pansy urged. 'Aren't
you longing to bathe?'

Atalanta took no notice, continuing to trail and recite in
a droning mumble, the lines all running into each other. '*To
whom the Romans pray, a Roman's life, a Roman's arms,
take thou in charge this day!*'

'She *is* a spy,' thought Pansy. She was saying it for a
reason, to someone who was listening – not Nonna, she

didn't think, although she could hear too – but to someone who was hiding. *Arms*, Atalanta was talking about arms! There was a blackberry bush on the edge of the track. Pretending she was picking blackberries, Pansy glared into it. Nobody's eye glared back at her; it was dense bushiness. There was nowhere else within hearing distance to hide. The down sloped up smoothly and then in wide gentle ledges like giant steps. There were sheep grazing on them. Atalanta wasn't a spy, nor was Nonna; she knew it really. But if they had been it would have been terrifying and exciting.

If *only* they would hurry. But Nonna, who had caught up with them, stopped again. Gazing up at the downs and sheep, she said, 'The lights are quite lovely. Look at those shadows...'

Pansy stopped to stare politely, but she couldn't bear to stop long. 'Please can I go on to the sea?'

'But of *course*, darling!' Nonna's gaze was still on the downs. 'I shall stay here I think and feast my eyes, and plan the picture I shall paint tomorrow.'

Can we bathe without you? Pansy did not say it but, before Nonna could say they couldn't, she cried, 'Come on, Atalanta!' and tore off down the track. Just before the bend she stopped and looked back. Atalanta wasn't running; she never ran. She had got a bit farther, but not much. Nonna had stopped feasting her eyes and was bent double, picking something. If she had been a sheep she would have been grazing, but she wasn't.

Round the bend, Pansy saw the sea – a blue triangle between the downs. Although she had expected it, it was the same lovely kind of surprise as finding a mushroom on the downs. The pale rocks came up to meet the grass. It was a small beach but it had everything: rocks, sand, pools. There was no one there. Basking in the hot evening sun, it seemed to be waiting for her.

With a little shriek of happiness, she clambered over the rocks. There was a pool shaped like a cup. The rock was very smooth and the water very clear. Wrenching off her sand-shoes, she dipped in her foot. How cool it was.

She let herself down into it, but it turned out much deeper than she had expected; the bottoms of everything were soaked. She ought to have held up her frock and petticoat and rolled up her drawers. It was the kind of accident Nana had meant, but she hadn't *fallen* in. Getting out, she sang 'Who cares!' to the tune of *While shepherds watched their flocks by night* which seemed to suit it, while she squeezed out her hems. She had just finished when she saw Atalanta. She was sitting on a rock looking as though she had been there for hours which Pansy knew well she hadn't been. 'Hullo! Isn't it lovely!' Pansy shouted.

If Atalanta made a sound it didn't carry. Pansy went over to her. 'There are the most scrumptious pools!' She could hardly talk fast enough to tell Atalanta about everything. 'How can you sit there like that?'

'Like what?'

'As though you were a hundred.'

'When I am a hundred I shan't sit here. I shall make my thirty-six grandchildren push me in a Bath chair to the top of the downs.'

'*Thirty-six!*'

'Not all at once; they'll have to have a rota, naturally.'

'It's too many, you can't have thirty-six.'

'Why not? – if all my six children have six children?' Detaching a piece of seaweed from a neighbouring rock, Atalanta tugged off one of the cushiony bits and sucked it.

'They'll hate you.'

'I don't mind.'

Atalanta was twelve – Pansy stared out to sea doing some arithmetic – 'You won't be a hundred for eighty-eight years. Look! – there's someone in the sea! Do you see that black thing bobbing out there? It's someone with dark hair.'

'It must be Nonna's dark handsome visitor coming from over the water,' said Atalanta.

'Is it? Is it?' cried Pansy excitedly.

Atalanta spat out the seaweed. 'No, of course it isn't; it's a bit of wood.'

Now Pansy could see that it wasn't a person. She felt bitterly disappointed and then suddenly it was a relief. They didn't want anyone else here; they wanted the beach to themselves, and Nonna wasn't here to be disappointed that it wasn't her dark handsome visitor.

They undressed to bathe, behind a rock. It was much more fun than the stuffy little hut you had on bigger beaches. Pansy's bathing-cap was pale green. When she pushed her hair into it it hung behind in a bag.

'What do you wear one for?' Atalanta said. 'I don't.'

'Your hair will get sopping and full of salt.' Pansy hesitated. She and Aunt Katie had been to buy hers specially. Nonna hadn't taken Atalanta. She said, 'Now I've got it on I'll keep it on.' It was meant as comfort, not to sound pleased with hers if Atalanta wanted one, but she wasn't sure Atalanta did. Atalanta might think her inartistic and undistinguished for wearing one, as *she* thought Atalanta dirty sometimes. She began blowing up her wings while Atalanta was still unbuttoning her Liberty bodice. Since Atalanta could swim she didn't need wings. Her parents sent her to a swimming-bath in London to get rid of her. Wasn't it beastly of them? Pansy had said to Grandfather, and Grandfather had said, 'No more beastly than you being sent up to the nursery to get rid of you, and a swimming-bath would be more exciting than the nursery, I imagine.' Watching Grandfather pinching the heart of a lettuce, a thought had struck Pansy. 'Do you think she meant they wanted her to drown?' Grandfather had stood up, bringing the lettuce with him. 'No, I don't; I think that by having her taught to swim they were trying to keep her from drowning and if she ever tells you anything different, tell her not to tell such confounded great whoppers.' Atalanta hadn't.

Atalanta and Pansy's wings were ready at the same moment. Atalanta's bathing-dress was blue alpaca with a sailor-collar. It was too big. The tunic came almost to her knees, although it was hunched up round her waist with a belt, and the legs came half-way down her calves. Pansy stared in astonishment. 'Is it your own?'

'No, Nonna's; mine's in London.' Taking off her spectacles, Atalanta laid them on a rock. Without them she had her groping look. She didn't grope because she could see enough to walk, but she looked as if she were going to.

They went down to the sand. Atalanta stumped straight into the sea as though it were a warm bath. She looked as though she was going in in all her clothes.

'You'll drown!' cried Pansy. 'Your dress will pull you under like the man Grandfather knew who plunged in in his macintosh.'

'Rot! – and it's not a macintosh.' Atalanta walked on till the water reached her chest. Then she began to swim. She swam with great sweeping lazy strokes. She didn't hold up her chin as Pansy did in case the sea got into her mouth; she let the sea splash in if it wanted to.

How Pansy would love to swim like that! When the sea had reached her waist, she put on her wings. She put the belt part round her chest and under her armpits and the two fat white air-cushions on either end bulged up behind her shoulder-blades. Splash – she was off! Her arms thrashed through the water much quicker than Atalanta's and her legs splashed about on their own. She was lying flat out in the water, not a toe on the ground. She couldn't sink with the wings, but last year she *had* kept up a minute without them.

3

GOB-STOPPERS AND A FIND

On Friday Nonna got a letter from Dorcas, her parlour-maid. Dorcas always wrote to her when she was away, and Nonna wished she wouldn't. When she was away she didn't want to know if there was a stain on one of the damask table-cloths, or a crack on the drawing-room ceiling.

'You don't mind,' said Atalanta. 'You wouldn't mind if the house fell down.'

'I wouldn't want it on top of me, naturally,' said her grandmother, 'as I haven't the faintest wish to be killed just at present, but I sometimes wish I lived in an enormous studio, uncluttered by furniture and maids.'

'Who would cook?' demanded Atalanta bluntly.

'No one. I should live on melons, cheese, Gentleman's Relish and coffee.'

'And dates,' added Atalanta, as though she found the whole thing quite natural.

What funny food, Pansy thought. She couldn't imagine the Aunts wanting to do that. They would be miserable if the house fell down. But Nonna was Bohemian. Pansy had heard Aunt Katie tell Nana so, and when Pansy had asked what *Bohemian* was, she had said 'Easy-going.' 'How easy-going?' Pansy had inquired and Aunt Katie had said, 'Oh, in many little ways, like – well, like letting Atalanta's fringe grow into her eyes, and so on.' Now, when Pansy suddenly remembered about Bohemian, she quite saw that this was why Nonna would like to live in a studio and eat so oddly.

'The sweep is coming to do the morning-room chimney,' said Nonna reading the letter. 'There's a bird's nest up there. Dorcas was very cross I wouldn't have it swept with the others in the spring, but of course I wouldn't till the birds had flown.'

'I don't think we had any nests,' said Pansy, disappointed. 'The sweep came to us. He told Florrie he weighs sixteen stone. He's absolutely *enormous*. Grandfather says he's wasted as a sweep, he ought to be a policeman.'

'That's the one,' said Nonna, 'Smith. Underneath the soot he's very good-looking. He's got the most enchanting smile.'

'He lives in River Lane,' said Pansy, 'and there's a plank across the stream to get to his front door.'

'Is he coming after we get back?' Atalanta asked.

'Yes, the following week, but you'll be in London by then.'

'Has he got dark hair?' Atalanta, who was making a good breakfast, helped herself to a great dollop of marmalade.

'Perhaps – I don't know. When I saw him he had a red scarf tied round his head like a pirate – it *had* been red at least, but it was very sooty.'

'He has got black hair,' Pansy said.

'Then it's him,' said Atalanta flatly.

'Who?' asked Pansy.

'Nonna's dark handsome visitor from over the water, of course.'

Nonna laughed, 'How clever of you! Yes, of course, that's it.'

'He can't be,' said Pansy slowly. 'It meant from over the sea, someone different and exciting, who was *staying*.'

'It didn't say *sea*, it said *water*, and it didn't say anything about being exciting or staying, it's only what you thought,' Atalanta told her.

Part of Pansy felt excited, wanting the fortune to be true, and the other part felt disappointed, wanting it to be different. 'Do you really think the fortune meant him?' she asked Nonna.

'Undoubtedly, I should imagine.'

'Are you sorry it isn't someone else?'

'No, not at all. I'm delighted. Uninvited visitors, unless they are close friends or very charming, can be rather tiresome at times.' Nonna smiled, 'Now my fortune is settled we'll have to wait and see what turns up for you and Atalanta. Atalanta must dig up some gold and you – what was yours exactly?'

Pansy knew it by heart. '*Do not be dismayed if you find yourself among strangers. Rely on your own resources and you will contrive to extricate yourself with a certain amount of difficulty.* I don't want it; it's beastly! I hate strangers!' she cried.

'Don't be ridiculous, dear child. Life is a long succession of meeting strangers – unless you're a hermit, and I don't think that would suit you at all. All your friends were strangers when you first met them and you may be going to meet a lifelong friend. It's a most enthralling prospect.'

In spite of what Nonna said, Pansy still didn't feel enthralled. 'I think I'm going to be alone among them.'

'Look out they don't scalp you. I don't think you're going to meet your best friend, but your worst enemy. If you ask me,' said Atalanta, 'it's a warning.'

'Perhaps –' agreed her grandmother vaguely. 'I must hurry, or I shall miss the light.'

When Nonna had gone off to catch the morning light on the downs with her canvas and her paint-box – she had left her easel and her camp-stool hidden in a blackberry bush yesterday – Atalanta and Pansy went up to the village shop.

Pansy bought five postcards; one each for Boggles and Ginie and Grandfather, one for Aunt Susu and Aunt Katie between them, and one for Nana. She got a picture of a lobster for Boggles. She got the downs for Grandfather, and the church for the Aunts, and a horse looking over a gate for Nana. For Ginie she got the beach. If Ginie was having an exciting time, she wouldn't be green with envy. She would ask her to keep it for her album. At tuppence each that was tenpence, and five halfpenny stamps was tuppence halfpenny. She only had sixpence pocket-money, but Grandfather had given her seven and six for emergencies, delicacies and entertainment, to be spent at her own discretion. He had not advised tipping at the farm; it might present a problem, he had said, and as she had a lifetime of tipping ahead of her there was no hurry to begin. If she wanted very much to give something to anyone at the farm, she could buy them a little present. 'And if you go anywhere where there are donkeys on the beach you might want to treat Atalanta to a ride,' he had suggested. At the thought of Atalanta on a donkey she and Grandfather had both laughed rather loudly.

After the postcards and stamps, Pansy bought two gobstoppers, one for Atalanta and one for herself. They cost a halfpenny each. Lastly, she got Atalanta a liquorice bootlace. If she gave her more than she'd got herself she hoped it would count as a proper good deed for the day although Grandfather had given her the money.

They started in on the gob-stoppers at once. They changed colour as you sucked, that was the exciting thing about them. Pansy kept on taking hers out to look at it. Atalanta kept hers in. Her cheek was so strained over it it looked as though she'd got a boil. When Pansy had hers in she looked as though she'd got one too. When she had taken it out for the third time, she said in amazement, 'Don't you want to look at yours? Mine's going pink.'

Atalanta said 'No,' and dribbled.

Going down the track they saw Nonna painting in the distance. Pansy waved and shouted but Nonna took no notice. Atalanta did nothing.

By the time they came to the bramble on the left, Pansy's gob-stopper, which had been absolutely pink at the last look, had already gone green. How wonderful it was! 'How *can* you not look at yours?'

'I know it's doing what yours is.' Atlanta had tied the liquorice bootlace round her neck. 'Guess who I am.'

'The Lamb.' Miss Lamb wore a black velvet band round her neck.

Atalanta nodded solemnly. She didn't even smile. Pansy, who would have liked not to smile either, laughed so uproariously that the gob-stopper fell out of her mouth and rolled down the track. Running after it, her hat fell off; stopping to pick it up, she lost sight of her sweet.

When Atalanta reached her, Pansy had stopped searching the track and was beginning on the grass at the side.

Atalanta poked about with the toe of her sand-shoe. Pansy crawled, searching with her hands. She heard a lot of chirping and then she saw it – a bright green grasshopper chirping its head off on the stem of a grass. 'Look!' But there was nothing to look at; it had gone. She had just pricked her finger on some rest-harrow, when Atalanta said, 'Ha! – look what I've got.'

How gorgeous, she'd found her gob-stopper! Pansy jumped up to get it, but instead of a lovely green ball in Atalanta's hand, there was a small flat brownish-grey thing. 'I thought you'd got it,' said Pansy, disappointed.

Atalanta was peering very closely at her hand. Then she spat on it and rubbed it with the hem of her frock. Then she peered again. She had made no effort to answer when Pansy had asked what it was, but now she said, 'Roman'.

'Is it a Roman coin?'

Atalanta nodded.

Pansy had seen lots of Roman coins in the museum at home but they hadn't interested her nearly as much as the pillory where thieves had stood with their head and hands pushed through holes in a wooden frame while people laughed and pelted them with rotten eggs. But seeing Roman coins in rows in a glass case was quite different from seeing one that Atalanta had just picked up. 'It's such a funny colour.'

'It's dirty – absolutely ingrained with the earth of centuries, but once I've got it cleaned I bet it turns out to be bronze.'

'Do you think the Roman legions passed this way?' Looking down the path, Pansy saw them with her mind's eye – Romans with shining breastplates and helmets tramping up from the sea. With her naked eye she saw the empty chalky track running between the downs. A blue butterfly fluttered past.

'Not necessarily,' said Atalanta. 'Any Roman could have dropped it. It got buried, I suppose, and now it's come to the surface again.'

How exciting it was to think of a Roman here, standing perhaps exactly where she was. And then the spell of the past suddenly fell from Pansy. Atalanta had got everything: her gob-stopper, the liquorice bootlace which was still round her neck, and the coin as well. 'You're dribbling,' she said, and then in a flash she realized – 'It's your *new-found riches!* What your fortune said!'

'No, it isn't. It meant money I could spend, English money or foreign currency that I could use.'

'It didn't say so. It said *your financial position is about to improve* and this is money whether you can spend it or not, so it has.'

'It said *Abstain from squandering your new-found riches*; how can I squander' – Atalanta pushed the gobstopper further into her cheek – 'money I can't spend?'

Pansy didn't know, but she felt certain this was Atalanta's fortune, which made her seem to have even more of everything. 'Perhaps, when it says *abstain from squandering,'* she said slowly, 'it means don't throw it away or lose it. I advise you to keep it carefully, whether you think it's your fortune or not, and you mustn't be *too proud to accept advice from a friend* and the friend *is* me.'

Atalanta had hooked the gob-stopper out of her cheek which was aching a bit with so much stretching. Now it was behind her front teeth. She swallowed spit. "If that's all the advice you can give me! Of course I shan't throw it away; as though I would.' Holding the coin close to her spectacles, she blinked at it. 'What an acquisition!'

Acquisition didn't sound as splendid as it might have, muffled by the gob-stopper, but it did sound rather splendid all the same. Pansy's envy increased. Atalanta had got an acquisition and her fortune whatever she said, and Nonna's was coming true too. It wasn't fair if theirs came true and hers didn't, but on the other hand she didn't want hers; she didn't want the enthralling prospect of going among strangers whatever Nonna said. And she *did* want her gob-stopper. 'Perhaps my gob-stopper's rolled the whole way to the beach.'

'It couldn't have; it could never have taken the corner. If you don't find it, you can have my bootlace if you like,' said Atalanta magnanimously.

No, Pansy couldn't; it had been a present and her good deed. If Atalanta gave it back she'd be taking away her good deed and doing one herself the way she'd done with the bed. No, it wasn't like the bed because she wouldn't have her good deed *and* the bootlace and with the bed she'd let Pansy keep her good deed. But as a matter of fact Pansy wasn't at all sure that she wanted the bootlace anyhow; Atlanta's neck was pretty hot and she hadn't washed it this morning because she'd bathed yesterday. 'Thanks awfully,' she said, 'but I'll find it, it must be somewhere.'

'Matter is indestructible,' said Atalanta, but this wisdom was of no use to Pansy, who had already started down the track again. It was there, in the middle of a rut, broken clean in half so that all the layers of colours showed – blue, pink, green, white, blue. You could see what happened when you sucked; there was no mystery any longer.

4

<hr>

SATURDAY'S EXPEDITION

On Saturday Nonna came down to breakfast in her green grass hat. It was the shape of a toadstool with no trimming of any kind. It always had been like that, she said, quite naked – unlike Atalanta's panama, which had once had a ribbon. You didn't need a hat with embellishments to paint in – just something untrammelled and shady. She had worn it every day after the day they arrived, but never for breakfast before. She was in a hurry to get to the churchyard to sketch the Norman porch before they set out for their expedition to Crackingbourne.

Pansy went with her. Atalanta went on reading. She had started reading *The Wide Wide World* in bed last night and gone on this morning. She had read all through breakfast. When Nonna had said, 'Are you coming with us?' Atalanta took no notice, and Nonna took no notice of Atalanta not noticing. 'Because if you are not,' she said, 'I think you should move from there presently so that Mrs Chubb can clear the breakfast.' Atalanta had moved to the horsehair sofa.

The churchyard grass had been scythed; there were wisps of hay lying about. Over the fence a Jersey cow chewed and swished its tail. Nonna put her camp-stool on the path close to a grave like a table. Pansy examined the writing on it, EBENEZER ELAM DOBBS, she read. There was a ladybird crawling on the o of DOBBS. 'How enchanting,' murmured Nonna when Pansy told her, but she didn't get up to look, she went on drawing. Pansy, who was accustomed to the inscriptions on the tablets in the cathedral at home, knew that *issue* meant children. Ebenezer and Abigail his wife

36

had had eight issue. Henry had died at two weeks, but
Emma Mary who had been born after him had lived to be a
hundred and three. Her relics were interred with those of
her husband, Captain Horatio Stubbings, in an adjoining
tomb. Pansy found the tomb inside a railing.

Nonna remarked that reading gravestones was rather like
making a patchwork quilt, picking up names and dates of
husbands and wives and children and grandparents and
gathering them all up together in the pattern of a family.
'I can see Ebenezer and his family quite plainly.'

'Can you?' said Pansy, dismayed. She looked round the
churchyard. There was a rustling in the yew tree but it
turned out to be a blackbird. The cow was still there
munching. A sudden thought struck her. 'Do you think
they'd count for the strangers in my fortune? It said not to
be dismayed if I find myself among strangers,' she added to
refresh Nonna's memory if it needed refreshing.

'No,' said Nonna, 'I'm sure your strangers will be alive,
besides, didn't it say something about extricating yourself

with difficulty? You can leave here any moment you want; there's no one here to stop you.'

No, of couse there wasn't and it was a relief, but on the other hand if the people these names belonged to could have counted, it seemed to Pansy for a moment that they'd have been better than living strangers. She said, 'I know. Grandfather says a churchyard is like a cloakroom where all the coats are empty because the people have gone away.'

Nonna agreed that that's how it was exactly. She was only seeing the Dobbs family with her mind's eye, nothing else. 'And now,' she said, 'I've made my sketch and we must hurry.' She arose in her trailing fashion but without hurrying. Pansy had never seen her hurry. Pansy carried the camp-stool back to the farm as she had carried it coming. It was her good deed being done and finished for the day.

Mr Chubb, the farmer, drove them to Crackingbourne in his gig; he always went in on market day, although today he was later than usual as he was not taking in any butter or eggs. He wasn't waiting to bring them back; they were coming on the 5.5 train. 'If we miss that we shall have to sleep on the beach,' Nonna said.

Nonna was much too old to sleep on the beach, Pansy knew. Aunt Katie said that although she dressed so gaily, Lavinia must be getting on for as old as she was. Pansy couldn't imagine Aunt Katie sleeping on the beach. 'What will you do if we have to?' Pansy asked. 'Shall we lie down on the sand?'

'No, I think it would be better to get deck-chairs – there are sure to be plenty for hire on a beach of that size – and settle down comfortably under the stars.'

It sounded such a natural, ordinary thing to do and as if Nonna would enjoy it. Pansy asked eagerly if they couldn't stay on purpose.

'I think not, darling. Our feet might get bitten by sandflies.'

'I don't think they bite at night,' said Atalanta, without looking up from *The Wide Wide World* which she was reading in the gig.

'You don't know what habits of a lifetime an insect will

break when tempted, any more than a human,' Nonna said, 'and they find feet just as succulent a delicacy as we find caviare and smoked-salmon, I expect.'

'I've never had either,' said Pansy.

'You poor darling, we must see what we can do!'

'I have and they're both beastly; I'd rather have new bread and pork dripping any day,' Atalanta said.

Just then Mr Chubb, who had forgotten something as they were starting, came back and got into the gig. He filled most of the space that was left.

The gig was enormous fun – much better than a stuffy old cab, Pansy thought; better than a carriage too, but not quite so exciting as Grandfather's car. Nothing was. The horse, a grey cob, took the narrow lane at a spanking trot. 'If anything comes we'll collide,' she said.

'Naught will,' said Mr Chubb as though he were a fortune-teller.

It was just on one o'clock by the time they had reached the parade at Crackingbourne and said goodbye to Mr Chubb. Mr Chubb took a watch out of his waistcoat pocket and compared it with the town clock on the parade. He was the only one of them who had a watch. Nonna, who had a small gold watch that pinned on to the front of her dress, had forgotten to pin it there, and Atalanta's had stopped yesterday. Pansy didn't possess one.

After the little cove at Longspit, this big fashionable beach seemed enormous, which as a matter of fact it was. There was a pier, and bathing-machines on wheels with steps going down into the sea, and tents as well. Those you could see at a glance, but there was a good deal more waiting to be discovered.

'We'll eat first and get rid of the food,' said Nonna, 'and then you two can bathe and amuse yourselves and I shall go and sketch the harbour.'

'We'll get cramp and drown if we bathe directly after eating,' Atalanta pointed out. She didn't sound as if she would mind drowning, she was simply imparting knowledge.

'Then don't; I'd prefer you not to drown,' said her grandmother easily. 'Let's stroll along and see where we'd like to sit.'

As they strolled Pansy caught sight of some donkeys. She could give Atalanta a ride, she thought, just as Grandfather had suggested. It would be a good deed because she *might* have spent all the money on herself, but she had done her deed for today. Perhaps it could be tomorrow's; it seemed a pity to waste it.

But Atalanta said she was too heavy for a donkey; she needed a horse.

There was a splendid sand-castle. The man who had made it had his cap on the sand for pennies. It was Windsor Castle. 'Windsor Castle is on a hill,' Atalanta told him.

'Aye missie, so be.'

'This isn't – you've put it flat on the ground.'

The man smiled and nodded as though Atalanta was a little child or a pleasant idiot.

'Why did you?' she persisted.

'That's roight.'

'It's *not*. It's idiotic to purposely make a thing wrong.' Grovelling in her pocket, she brought out a penny and dropped it severely into his cap. Pansy had nothing between sixpence and a halfpenny. She gave him the halfpenny and said she was sorry it wasn't more. When she caught her up, Atalanta said it was silly to be sorry when he hadn't bothered to dig a hill.

Nonna had got left behind. She had stopped in the middle of the beach. 'Dreaming,' said Atalanta laconically and sat down exactly where she stood to wait for Nonna to arrive. She started to read again.

Nonna sat on her camp-stool for the picnic and Pansy and Atalanta sat on the sand. Deck-chairs were all right if you were spending the night on the beach, but if you were having a picnic you wanted to be a little more Bohemian, Nonna said. No one said, 'What's Bohemian?' Atalanta knew everything and Pansy knew this too. She quite saw how much more easy-going it was to sit on a camp-stool or the sand.

They had sandwiches with cold beef in them, and lettuce

and tomatoes and jam tarts and cheese and biscuits and lemonade. When they had reached the tart stage, Pansy caught sight of a horse being led down to the sea. 'Look, Atalanta – there's a horse for you to ride!'

'It's going to pull out the machines.' Atalanta's voice was muffled with food.

'Yes, the tide's going out fast,' said Nonna. 'The steps are high and dry.'

'Why can't the bathers walk into the sea, when the people from the tents have to walk the whole way down the beach?' Pansy said.

'Because they don't want to traipse along exposed to the vulgar gaze, presumably.' Nonna paused to flick a little piece of pastry off her lap. 'And also because they want a quick immersion – less of a creep in.'

The machines were very heavy; the horse had to tug dreadfully.

When they had finished eating Nonna said, 'Now I'm going to the harbour. I shall be back in plenty of time to catch the train. I'll meet you – where shall I meet you?'

'Under the clock,' said Atalanta. 'When?'

'When I'm there,' said Nonna vaguely, gathering up her stool.

Atalanta started to read again. Pansy went off to paddle. It was all sand and very shallow with tiny little waves coming in with big gaps between them. When they broke it looked like frills of lace. She saw a fat man in white flannels and a blazer and a straw hat go up the ramp at the back of one of the machines. While she waited for him to come out of the front, she paddled out a bit. It wasn't one of the shelving beaches, you could see it wasn't by the people bathing. It was so shallow you'd have to go miles to drown, she thought. When the fat man came down the steps in a black and white striped bathing-suit, the water was only half-way up his calves in spite of the horse. Wrapping his arms round his chest, he pummelled his shoulder blades; next he bent double and sloshed the sea up into his face; then he plunged forward and threw himself flat on his front and came up snorting and shaking his head like a dog

– the snorts carried back to Pansy who had paddled out as far as she could.

She went back to the edge of the sea then and wandered along till she came upon the children. There were a lot of them scattered over the beach, boys and girls. The girls had on grey frocks and brown sun-bonnets and black stockings and boots. The boys had grey jerseys and corduroy shorts and black stockings and boots. How dreadfully hot they must be. Why didn't they paddle? Even if they were digesting they could paddle. It must be a school, she thought, and then remembered it was holidays. It must be a home. One of the boys was kneeling with his back to her. There was something written on the back of his jersey. Going nearer, trying to pretend she wasn't staring, Pansy saw what it was; it was WORKHOUSE. She did stare then in shocked dismay, but after a moment turned and walked back into the sea.

5

STOCKINGS AND BOOTS

Pansy knew all about the Workhouse. She had never forgotten what Florrie had said that day when she was cleaning silver in the pantry, how a self-respecting person would rather die than go there, and old people went because they hadn't been able to die, and orphans because they couldn't help it. Grandfather had agreed it wasn't a place people wanted to go to, except tramps: they didn't mind because they didn't stay except perhaps for a night or two; they went to get food – and boots if they were lucky – in return for a job of work. There had got to be Workhouses for the destitute – where else would they go? – and they couldn't be extravagant places because there wasn't the money, but there was no reason why they shouldn't be run with kindness, Grandfather had said. Some were, but some, he was afraid, left a good deal to be desired, and the sooner they were reformed the better. 'They need a thorough investigation.' He had sounded rather as though he were talking to himself, not Pansy. 'Can't someone give them a thorough investigation?' she had asked, and Grandfather had said that it wasn't always easy for an outsider, yet it was an outsider that was often needed to get to the root of things and find out exactly what was happening.

Standing in the sea up to her ankles, Pansy's face, which had become scarlet with shock, slowly went back to its proper colour, but she still felt dreadful. It seemed so awful that all those children should be in the Workhouse, and not only that but that they should have it written on their backs. It wasn't *fair*! How could they bear those woollen

43

stockings and boots? They had to because they weren't allowed to take them off, that's why, it must be.

One of the boys who looked about seven, like Boggles, ran towards the sea and threw in a stone. His boots went in the water. A girl came after him. 'It's over yer boots, Jo – yer won't 'arf cop it! Yer don't wants another tannin' does yer?'

'Naw –' Jo shot a glance up the beach, then running away, knelt down and scuffed up the sand with his hands like a dog.

Pansy and the girl stared at each other. The girl's face was covered all over in freckles; it looked like a robin's egg. She had green eyes like Snodgrass, the Archdeacon's cat. Pansy envied her; she'd love to have eyes like Snoddy. As she looked they changed from green to brown as Snoddy's did. The girl's sun-bonnet had slipped off the back of her head. Her hair was strained back so tightly – she hadn't a snood – it looked rather as though it were pulling her eyelids with it.

'Aren't you allowed to paddle?' Pansy asked.

'Naw.'

'Why?'

' 'Cos we b'aint.'

'Don't you want to?'

'Not 'arf I don't.' Sucking in her lips, she looked at the sea.

'Haven't you ever paddled?'

' 'Course I 'as,' she said scornfully. 'I can swim too. Granfer said I oughter bin a fish.'

There was a small silence. Pansy wanted to say 'Where is your grandfather?', but guessing he was dead she didn't. She said, 'I can't swim quite – at least I did for a minute last year.' She said it to comfort, but the girl ignored it.

' 'E said I oughter bin a boy then I could 'ave bin a fisherman like 'im.'

'Would you have liked that?'

'Liked it? Wotcher think?'

Pansy felt silly. 'Why aren't you allowed to bathe or paddle?'

'Cos we b'aint.'

Pansy knew that by now but she still wanted to know why. She decided to leave it however for the moment. 'It isn't fair, it's *beastly* not to let you – not to let you paddle, anyway.' Looking down at the girl's thick black woollen stockings and boots, she said, 'Why don't you paddle? If you had just a little quick paddle no one might see.'

'They'd see!'

'Who's they?'

'Long Nose and 'er.'

'Who are they?'

' 'E's Master and 'er's Matron.'

'Where are they?' Pansy stared up the beach in the direction where Jo had looked.

The girl hitched her sun-bonnet back on her head, but she didn't look. 'Up there, sittin' in the chairs.'

There were quite a lot of people dotted about in deckchairs, but Pansy guessed it was the two in the distance by the parade, and then as she looked she was sure of it; she saw the man beckon to a Workhouse boy who ran to him. 'I see,' she said. 'They're a long way away, and if I stood behind you they mightn't see you, if you were quick and if they did you'd have done it before they could stop you and you'd have had the fun. I would,' she urged.

'An' get shut up?'

'Shut up, where?'

'In a dark cupboard all day an' night without grub.'

'They couldn't shut you up all night,' said Pansy, appalled.

'Aw couldn't they just! A lot yer knows!' the girl said scornfully.

Pansy felt ashamed at not knowing more, as though she was to blame for not having been treated in this awful way too. 'Would they do that to you if you only *paddled*?'

'Not 'arf they wouldn't.'

Pansy looked up the beach again. It was too far to see their faces and she didn't want to.

The girl turned abruptly and walked away. She hadn't got WORKHOUSE on her back. Then Pansy saw another girl who hadn't either; only the boys had it, she supposed. She watched the girl crouch down by Jo. She might have said good-bye, she thought crossly. Finding fault with her helped Pansy to feel less sorry for her, which was more comfortable. But she still felt dreadfully unhappy about her, and all the others, too, in their boots and stockings. The day seemed spoilt. She longed to tell Nonna and Atalanta. Surely Nonna would be able to do something to help when she got back from the harbour – like speaking to Long Nose. And perhaps Atalanta would have a plan. Just then she heard Atalanta's voice behind her. 'Do come on, I've got a tent.'

'A tent?' said Pansy stupidly.

'Yes, you know people aren't allowed to undress on the beach, they never are on big public beaches. I've brought your bundle.'

'Thanks awfully.' Pansy followed as Atalanta started to plod towards the row of tents. 'You see that girl kneeling with that boy?' she whispered. 'I've been talking to her.'

'What about?'

'I'll tell you in the tent. You see that man and woman sitting up by the parade –'

'No,' said Atalanta.

No, she wasn't interested was what she meant, Pansy thought, but she would be when she had told her what she knew. On their way they passed one of the boys.

'I can't think why they have to label them like jam.' Atalanta said.

'Jam?' Pansy hadn't thought of *jam*.

The narrow white canvas tent, in the row of tents which all looked exactly the same, was number 6. There were laces to close the flaps, but Atalanta hadn't bothered to tie them after dumping their bundles on the sandy wooden floor. There was a small bench which the bundles were meant to go on, but she hadn't bothered about putting them on that either. Crowded into the dim stuffy little space inside the tent, Pansy told Atalanta everything.

'Workhouses are known to be awful,' Atalanta said. 'If they weren't, all the lazy ne'er-do-weels would want to crowd into them.'

'The children can't help it – *they* aren't lazy ne'er-do-weels.' Pansy dragged off her vest. 'They're orphans.'

'Not always. The sins of the fathers are visited on the children,' said Atalanta stolidly.

'She never mentioned her father; it was her grandfather who said she ought to have been a fish.'

'Then ten to one her father was a wash-out unless he died when she was a baby. Did she refer to her mother?' asked Atalanta, dropping her drawers on the floor.

No, now Pansy came to think about it, she hadn't. She said 'No,' reluctantly; she didn't want it to look as though the girl's mother had been a ne'er-do-weel, it might make Atalanta less sorry for her. She wanted Atalanta to be so sorry she would think of some way to help.

'Of course her mother may have died when she was born,' said Atalanta judiciously.

'Then she's an orphan if her father's dead too.'

'That doesn't mean they weren't ne'er-do-weels, and that her grandfather wasn't one too. If they weren't and they're all dead, why didn't they leave her provided for?'

Provided for – how splendidly grown-up it sounded.

47

thought Pansy admiringly. 'Perhaps her grandfather's fishing boat was wrecked and went down with him and everything that had been provided on it.'

'Don't be silly.' Atalanta's voice came muffled from inside Nonna's bathing-dress as she pulled the tunic over her head. 'He wouldn't have had his furniture and everything on board. Anyway,' she said as her head came out of the neck, 'she's in the Workhouse and that's that, and she's no worse off than the others – except that she wants to paddle and if the others never have they mayn't miss it. She's made her choice between cupboard and not paddling and she's chosen not paddling. There's nothing more to be done.'

'But she's *cruelly treated*!' said Pansy.

'Paupers often are,' said Atalanta, removing her spectacles. 'What else do they do to them besides starving them in a cupboard?'

'Tanning. Jo – he looked about Boggles' age – got his boots wet and she said if they'd seen him, he'd have had another tanning. It sounded,' said Pansy unhappily, 'as if he's had a good many already.'

'Quite likely, if he goes on doing things he's not allowed to and getting found out; that's not cruelty,' said Atalanta brutally.

'I think it's cruelty to be on the beach on a boiling day and not even allowed to paddle and to have *Workhouse* on your back,' said Pansy slowly.

'It's worse than having it on the front, I admit. On the front, you could at least wrap your arms round it and hide it if necessary. Come on if you're coming.' Atalanta thrust her way out of the tent.

As the tents were right up by the parade, they had a long way to traipse to the sea exposed to the vulgar gaze. Pansy, who felt ashamed of being able to bathe as she had been for not having been shut up in a cupboard, longed for a quick immersion. She didn't want the Workhouse girl to see her, but she was there by Jo still, standing up looking towards the sea. 'She's there where she was,' Pansy breathed. 'I don't want her to see me as she can't bathe.'

48

'What's the good of two people not bathing because one can't?'

'I know,' said Pansy unhappily, 'but it's awful for her to see me. Pehaps if I don't look at her she won't recognize me. I think I'll run.' She rushed straight on into the sea. When she had waded till the water was over her knees, she looked back. The girl was still standing there watching. 'I bet she knew it was me,' thought Pansy, but she was probably watching Atalanta now, who was just coming in. Pansy waited for her.

'We'll be on the Continent before the water's up to our waists,' Atalanta complained. She looked blinky and odd as she always did without her spectacles.

'She's coming down now to the edge of the sea,' said Pansy. 'Do you see her?'

'Oh, do stop telling me where she is! I've seen her twice already. And I couldn't see her now without my specs if I wanted to – which I don't – if she was an elephant.'

'Couldn't you really see an elephant?' said Pansy.

'I could see a grey lump, I suppose.' Atalanta waded on and Pansy followed. When the water was half-way up her thighs, Pansy ducked. She had a good swim with her wings and a little one without because the beach was flat, but her knees scraped the sand almost at once.

Atalanta, who had plodded on a bit before she ducked, called, 'I've had an idea.'

'What?' Pansy started wading again.

'About that girl,' said Atalanta when they met. 'Change clothes with her – she's about your size – and she can paddle. Long Nose will never know the difference from right up the beach – as long as he doesn't see you both go in or come out of the tent, of course. You'll have to do it separately. She'll have to sneak in, and when you've got her clothes on you'll have to sneak out.'

Pansy stared at Atalanta, her eyes shining with excitement, 'What a spiflicating idea!' Atalanta didn't look excited at all. She hadn't been able to duck-dive, it was too shallow, and although her pigtail was wet she still looked composed and as solid as a post. Pansy looked back at the girl; she was still on the edge. 'She can have my bathing-dress and bathe!' she cried excitedly.

'I shouldn't think she'd want to.'

'She does; I told you, she longs to!'

'Not in your sopping bathing-dress.'

'There's nothing else,' said Pansy, damped.

'Offer it by all means.' Atalanta lay back in the water and began to float. With her eyes shut her whole face seemed shut up too.

'You look dead,' Pansy said.

'I don't. I look like the Lady of Shalott floating down to Camelot.'

That was a poem by Tennyson, Pansy knew well. She had read the whole of it to Aunt Susu one wet afternoon. It was in four parts and at the end Aunt Susu had given her four chocolate beans, one for each part. It had taken ages. But Pansy had no time for poety now, so she did not point out that, unlike Atalanta, the Lady of Shalott had floated *in a boat* to Camelot.

Turning, she started to wade, with a great swishing of water, as quickly as she could towards the shore. How awful if the girl went away before she got there; and just as she'd thought this, the girl did turn and started to walk slowly along the beach, kicking the sand as she went. 'Don't go, please don't go!' Pansy felt as though she had said it aloud. She hadn't, which was a good thing because a woman in a bathing-cap with a scarlet bow was wading towards her and might have thought her mad. But as if the girl on the beach had heard, she now turned back towards the sea, and picking up a stone hurled it in.

Pansy reached the shore in time; the girl was still there and she was staring. 'It's me,' said Pansy eagerly. 'Listen, I've had the most splendid idea, at least –' No, she wouldn't say it was Atalanta's idea except about the bathing; the girl didn't know who Atalanta was for one thing – 'we'll change clothes and then I can hang about on the beach doing what you're doing and they'll think I'm you, and you can put on my clothes and paddle or – you can have my bathing-dress, if you don't mind it being wet, and bathe.'

The girl, who had been staring at her open-mouthed, said nothing for a moment; then she said rather breathlessly, 'Naw, not likely.'

'Oh, do!' said Pansy beseechingly. 'Think how you'd love to be in the sea again.'

'An' be killed if they found out. That's what they'd do, kill me.'

'No, they couldn't; they aren't allowed to murder by law. Surely you know that?' It was Atalanta. Pansy turned to find her just behind.

'I didn't know you were coming. This is Atalanta, a friend,' Pansy explained. 'It was really she who suggested it –' she said honestly, 'about changing clothes and paddling, I mean – but I thought of the bathing part.'

'Gertie was killed,' the girl said as though Pansy hadn't spoken. 'They killed her.'

'How?' Atalanta demanded.

'She fell outer winda.'

'If they didn't push her they didn't murder her. Did they push her?'

''Oo's ter knaw,' said the girl darkly.

'You've got to have proof before you can lay a crime at someone's door,' said Atalanta firmly. 'But it's no good fussing about that now. They won't kill you; they wouldn't dare if they've killed one already – which I bet you a shilling they haven't. There'd be talk. Now's your chance to get those boots and stockings off, and if you're going to accept Pansy's offer and have a bit of fun, you'd better get going   the less you're seen talking to us the better –' Atalanta blinked up the beach in the direction of Long Nose, 'and if they're where I think they are they've got a jolly good view of us, if they aren't asleep.'

'They don't never sleep.'

'Nonsense, they'd die if they didn't, and two minuses make a plus anyway.'

Pansy was quite sure the girl didn't know what *two minuses make a plus* meant. Atalanta meant that *don't never* meant *do*, but she didn't explain; she had more

important fish to fry just now than explaining grammar. 'You *would* like to paddle, wouldn't you?'

The girl nodded, 'Not 'arf I wouldn't.'

'Then come up to the tent and change,' urged Pansy.

'No,' said Atalanta; she had turned her back on them and was facing the sea, 'you mustn't go together, it will let the cat out of the bag at once. Go off, Pansy, and then you' – she didn't look round – 'can follow slowly as though you aren't going anywhere in particular. Sneak into the tent when no one's looking, it's number six. When you come out,' Atalanta was still giving her instructions in the direction of the sea, 'you can come out boldly in Pansy's clothes, and Pansy, you must sneak out like I told you.' But Pansy had already gone.

The girl said, 'Yes, miss,' and suddenly sucked in her breath.

When Pansy was in the tent she held the flap together hoping it would look as though she'd tied it, and peered through a slit. She saw the girl coming and Atalanta going back into the sea. If only she wouldn't look as though she was coming, but in spite of what Atalanta had said she did rather, 'Or perhaps it's because I *know*,' Pansy thought. She could hardly bear the suspense. When the girl was quite close, and Pansy couldn't see anyone looking, she thrust her face through the tent flap and hissed, 'Here –'

The girl saw her, glanced around, and then shot like a rat into the tent through the opening which Pansy made ready.

'Good,' said Pansy, tying the tapes with fumbling fingers. With her mind's eye she saw a long red nose poke between them. 'What colour's Long Nose's nose?' she asked.

'Yaller.'

Yellow seemed worse than red. 'Do you think they saw you coming?'

' 'Ope not. If they did I'm as good as dead.'

Pansy wished she hadn't asked. 'No, you aren't – you know what Atalanta said. Come on, give me your clothes.' Pansy suddenly had an idea, 'I can wear my own underclothes, they won't show.' While the girl was dragging off her frock she peeped again to see if anyone was coming, but

53

the coast seemed clear. When she looked again, the girl's frock was off. She didn't seem to have a petticoat. She had calico drawers and a grey woollen vest. Grey *wool*? How glad Pansy was she hadn't got to put on that! She wanted to say '*Why do you wear a grey woollen vest in the middle of the summer?*' but she didn't because she knew she had to: that's what she was given and there was nothing else she could wear. She said, 'Aren't you hot?' and without waiting for an answer said, 'Why don't you *bathe*? It's much more fun than paddling, especially as you can swim like a fish, though it's pretty shallow at the moment. I can give you the bathing-dress in a jiffy and it's drier than it was. Wouldn't you like to?'

The girl swallowed, 'Not 'arf.'

'Goodie.' Pansy took off her bathing-dress under her towel. 'Here you are.'

While she was dressing Pansy said, 'What's your name?'

'Leah Budden.'

Leah? Pansy had never met anyone called Leah before. 'Are you called after Leah in the Bible?'

'Dunno.'

'I'm Pansy Harcourt and I'm ten.' How old are you?'

' 'Leven.'

When Pansy put on the frock it was damp. She knew why: Leah *had* been hot. Being wet from the sea, like her bathing-dress was much nicer than being wet from being hot. The frock was very long, halfway down her legs, the way it had been on Leah. The stockings were damp too. As she put them on Pansy puffed air out of her nose instead of sniffing it up and tried not to look as though she minded. 'I think we ought to hurry,' she said, pulling up a garter. 'How long will you be here? – the Workhouse on the beach, I mean.'

'It's all dependin', but they won't be a'goin' not yet awhile.'

'Good – but the sooner you get into the sea the better. My bathing-dress looks all right on you and there's my cap. My hair's a little darker than yours but not much, and it's not plaited so tightly. I think we'd better leave it, but I've got a ribbon on and you've only got string.' That sounded rather rude but she hadn't meant it to. 'I expect string stays on better,' she added kindly. 'Give it to me can you? But I don't think you need put on my ribbon; you can shove everything up into my cap.'

When Leah was ready she looked like Pansy except for her face. Her body was about the same size although she was eleven.

'You go first and don't stop for anything,' Pansy said. 'Go straight into the sea; once you're there no one can stop you bathing.' She felt like Atalanta while she arranged things. 'Oh, I do hope you have a lovely time!'

Leah smiled suddenly so that her whole face changed and looked quite different. 'I 'opes so too.'

Pansy undid the flap of the tent and peered out. 'It's all right, go on –'

Leah, whose face had sharpened again into watchfulness, thrust aside the flap and bolted. Watching her run, Pansy suddenly felt the way she had when Grandfather let out a bird from the strawberry nets.

6

AMONG STRANGERS

When Pansy came out of the tent she wanted to run too, to get as far away as she could from Long Nose and Matron as quickly as possible, but she knew she mustn't. She did hurry a little to get away from the tent and then, keeping well away from the other Workhouse children, she walked towards the sea, dawdling a bit as she had seen Leah do. When she got to the edge, she picked up a stone as Leah had and threw it in.

Leah, who had waded very fast, had dipped now and was swimming. Nobody, not even *they*, could alter the fact that she'd bathed, thought Pansy triumphantly. Leah was cool now and clean and salty all over. Pansy, who had been all these things a little time ago, was hot. Her legs felt horrible in the stockings: hot, stuffy, itchy, and dirty. She never wore woollen stockings in the summer and no stockings at all since she'd been by the sea and allowed to be Bohemian. The frock was hateful too, but how glad she was she had kept on her own underclothes. She didn't know how she could have lived in that grey woollen vest. But nothing mattered really because the plan was working beautifully. Now Atalanta was swimming towards Leah. Pansy looked round to see that no one from the Workhouse was coming near her. They weren't, only someone in a white coat and skirt and white kid boots with a slobbering bulldog. Pansy looked back at the sea. She didn't want to speak to anyone, although if things had been different she would have liked to have looked closer at the bulldog.

Atalanta and Leah were standing up talking now for all to see. 'Now Leah looks like me,' thought Pansy, 'they can

of course.' It *was* them, she was sure, but they were so far
away by now, and there were such a lot of other people in
the sea, it wasn't easy to pick them out. It was them. Now
Atalanta had turned, Pansy recognized the sailor-collar of
Noona's bathing-dress. She wished she was with them,
standing safely out to sea, talking, able to see what they
were doing without danger. Part of her felt envious and left
out and abandoned, and the other part felt excited by the
danger; by her bravery, and by the thought that they
would be watching her to see what happened – no, Atalanta
couldn't see so far without her spectacles; Leah would have
to tell her. Pansy didn't like standing with her back to the
enemy, but it wouldn't be wise to stand with her face to
them. How awful if someone saw her plait was darker and
wasn't tight enough, how awful if her legs were fatter than
Leah's. Was that why the garters felt so tight?

A hand clawed at Pansy's dress. 'Yer gotter go up.' Without thinking, Pansy looked round. It was a Workhouse boy.
'Cor lumme!' His mouth fell open. 'Yer b'aint Leah.'

It was a great shock to Pansy. Fancy looking round and
letting the cat out of the bag straight off. She hadn't time to
wonder what she would have done if she hadn't looked
round and he hadn't seen her face. She said, 'No.'

'Wotcher a'doin' of in them things? Where's Leah?'

If the boy hated *them*, he'd be glad, Pansy decided. 'In
the sea in my bathing-dress,' she said truthfully. 'I lent it to
her to have a good bathe. When she's had it' – her eyes,
scanning the sea, couldn't pick up Leah or Atalanta for
certain at the moment; she thought they must be swimming again, but she did wish they were looking, that Leah
was and telling Atalanta what was happening – 'she'll put
on her own clothes again and I shall put on mine,' Pansy
finished.

'Leah b'ain't in the sea!' said the boy disbelievingly.

'Yes, she be – is. It's a secret, you mustn't tell a soul.'

'She won't 'arf cop it.' His pale face looked awed as he
turned his eyes from the sea to Pansy.

'It's a secret,' she repeated. 'Promise not to tell anyone.'

' 'Er wants yer, yer gotter go.'

'Who's 'er?' but Pansy knew. It was Matron, up there with Long Nose. She was too afraid to look round. She looked at the sea, longing for Atalanta who was beyond calling distance, even if she had dared to call.

' 'Er's Matron. 'Er seed yer come outer that tent arter yer bin a'stealin'.'

'*Stealing?*' said Pansy in astonishment. No sooner was the word out of her mouth than she received a violent box on the ears. She had never had them boxed before and for a moment, stupefied with surprise and pain, she did not realize what had happened.

'I'll teach you to go creeping into tents stealing, you skulking little pauper! Hand it over.'

Pansy blinked up at the woman who had come to stand in front of her.

'You aren't Leah! Who are you! What are you doing in those clothes? Where's Leah?'

Pansy lowered her head as the tears fell out of her eyes. She wasn't crying; her lips were trembling but she was biting the lower one to keep it still. The pain was getting less. She wiped her eyes quickly with her hand.

'Where's Leah? – Answer me.'

Pansy looked up, not at the woman she knew must be Matron, but at the sea. She had seen the woman's face and she couldn't look again yet. 'In the sea,' she said.

'The *sea*! The wicked, deceitful little wretch. I'll give her sea! Where is she?'

'Out far.'

'It's the last time *she'll* ever come near the sea! How dare she make you wear her clothes!'

Pansy saw a small stuffy pitch-dark cupboard with Leah in it; she had got to say it; she hadn't got to mention Atalanta either. 'She didn't, it was my idea.'

'Yours? So it was yours was it? You interfering little brat! Where's your mother?'

'In India.'

'Don't you sauce me. You think just because you aren't a pauper you can do as you like – I'll show you you can't.'

Pansy saw the cupboard with herself in it now, but

58

Matron couldn't shut *her* in it; she wasn't a Workhouse child. She could, she could drag her back there with her. There was no one to stop her. Atalanta was in the sea and Nonna in the harbour. Pansy felt quite sick with fright. And then she remembered something that she had once been told about bullies: that bullies were invariably cowards. Matron was a bully and if she was a coward it ought to be easy to answer her, but it wasn't easy at all.

'I wanted her to enjoy herself.' Pansy looked up reluctantly at the fat white face with the little nose like a thimble in the middle, at the black moustache which was so dreadful, the small eyes like black currants, and the frizzy black fringe just visible under the black straw bonnet. Gathering all her courage, she said what ought to daunt Matron if she was a coward, 'Why shouldn't she bathe? Why shouldn't they paddle? I think it's *beastly* not to let them.'

'Beastly, do you?' Matron's voice had a grating sound and her chin trembled. It wasn't trembling because she was going to cry, it was an angry tremble, Pansy was sure. She knew with fear and dismay that Matron wasn't daunted. 'Beastly – I'll teach you to say *beastly* to me.' Matron's voice rose. 'You wait till Master hears about this!'

Pansy didn't want to wait, but Matron's hand had fastened on her arm. 'Come along.'

Caught, terrified, Pansy looked at the sea. She thought she could see Atalanta, but without her spectacles Atalanta couldn't see her, couldn't see the awful thing that was happening. She couldn't see Leah who, if she was looking, *could* see what was happening. She did hope she was, that she would tell Atalanta who would know what to do. 'Please let me go and change,' Pansy said. She would feel so much better in her own frock and sand-shoes.

'Oh no, you don't!' Matron gave her a vicious tug. 'And don't you start a scene or I'll call the police.'

Pansy couldn't shriek. She shrieked when she was being chased in a nightmare and she had shrieked when she found a spider on her bed, but she couldn't shriek now in the middle of a crowded beach. They passed people sitting in deck-chairs. An elderly lady, who was thin and haughty-looking, glanced at her from under her purple parasol. 'I cannot think why they bother to bring those Workhouse children to the beach; they have a perfectly adequate yard,' Pansy heard a man growl from under his tilted Panama hat, as she was pulled along. A nurse, sitting on a rug with a baby, smiled at her kindly. *'Save me,'* Pansy might have implored, but she didn't. She didn't even smile back. Then the Matron put her foot in the moat of an abandoned sand-castle and stumbled, but instead of letting go of Pansy she clutched her harder.

They were there; they had stopped in front of a man in a chair. The man was Long Nose. His nose was very long and thin and it was rather yellow, and pinching the bridge of it was a pair of *pince-nez*. There were no hairs on his face and the thin strands on his head were brushed straight back. His long thin legs in black trousers were like hairpins.

'You won't credit what this child and that wicked Leah have done,' Matron said.

'What have they done, Matron?' asked Long Nose softly. Pansy, who had expected him to shout and be angry felt a great relief.

'Changed clothes, have you ever heard the like? Such underhand goings-on. Leah's in the sea, *bathing*.' *Bathing* sounded the most dreadful word when Matron said it.

'Why should they want to do that, I wonder?' He spoke gently as though he were quite mystified, looking up at Matron for an answer.

'She loves bathing. She used to bathe a lot before –' Pansy stopped, abashed. *Before she went into the Workhouse*, she had meant to say, but it would sound a little rude, she decided.

Matron, who had a bite on her neck, let go of Pansy's arm to scratch it. Pansy was very glad and relieved. How she hated her. But now she had seen Long Nose and found how gentle he was, everything was different. She couldn't understand why Leah hated him so; he couldn't help what his nose was like. He would never shut anyone up in a cupboard; it must be Matron. She would. 'And if she tries to take me away and shut me in, I'll ask him to stop her,' Pansy thought.

'How friendly of her to take such an interest in a poor little Workhouse child –'

Pansy warmed to him even more when he said that, but she did wish he wouldn't behave as though she weren't there; why didn't he look at her? But sometimes Nonna didn't seem to see people when she was thinking about her painting, and he was still wondering about Leah bathing. 'Why can't they all bathe?' she said. 'It's so lovely. If they haven't got bathing things I know they can't now, but they could all paddle.'

'Who is this child?' he asked. Turning his head he looked full at Pansy. 'Who are you, you meddling conceited little chit?' His voice lashed out at her like a whip, his pale eyes behind the glasses were piercing and venomous.

Appalled, disbelieving, Pansy stood stock-still for a moment, her feet, in Leah's boots, rooted to the sand. Then, terrified almost out of her wits, she began to run.

7

ALL AMONG THE MEAT

Pansy ran without plan, like running in a nightmare. She leapt a sand-castle and skirted a picnic party just in time. Seeing steps on to the parade, she dashed up those. She ran helter-skelter down the parade, past a Bath chair, past seats with people on them, past a man selling buckets and spades, bolting past other pedestrians, swerving to avoid a dog, swerving to avoid an old man, bolting on.

Then she heard the clatter of boots behind her above the noise of her own – or rather Leah's – boots. Glancing round, she saw two Workhouse boys in pursuit. One of them shouted something which she didn't hear. She must hide! She bolted across the street without looking to see if anything was coming, straight under the noses of two dray horses.

'Look where ye be a'goin, missie!' shouted the drayman, and then, seeing Pansy's clothes, said, 'One of they from the Poor'ouse, runnin' away, poor liddle varmint an' I shouldn'a be s'prised.' Then he saw the boys. 'Sent ter catch 'er an' take 'er back to be skinned alive – not over my dead body or my name's not Ben Stokes they won't.' Pulling up the dray, he blocked the boys. 'Don't ye go a'chasin' 'cross like that – straight under me 'orses' feet! Wot ye be at lads?'

'We gotter nab 'er!'

'Oh no, ye 'aven't. Mind yer own affairs and 'er'll mind 'ers.'

Pansy raced on. She was so out of breath and her legs ached so badly she couldn't run any more. The door of a butcher's shop stood wide open. The shop was empty. Darting in, she dropped on her hands and knees behind the counter. It was hollow. She crawled in between a tin and a box, panting like a dog. Her head was just above the tin which was half full of something red and slimy. There was blood on the sawdust on the floor. Then she heard feet running past, the feet of the boys. She had escaped! Suddenly she remembered her fortune; *it had happened!* She had been among strangers, worse ones than she had even thought of, and extricated herself with a certain amount of difficulty, and while it was happening she hadn't realised. *Do not be dismayed*, it had said, but she *had* been a bit, she couldn't help it. She was glad it had come true, she needn't go on not liking the thought of it any more. She had relied on her own resources and extricated herself, she thought again proudly, and now she must go before the butcher came. Where? She couldn't go back to the beach. She must go to the harbour and find Nonna. She was just about to crawl out when the butcher came.

He came round the back of the counter. He had black boots, and grey trousers, and Pansy could see the bottom of his blue and white striped apron. Afraid to breathe, she watched his boots turn round and take a step away from the counter towards the wall; she saw his heels come off the ground a little. He was reaching for something, he was reaching for meat off a hook. When he had got it, his boots came sideways again and walked away and Pansy heard a thump. She guessed what it was – the meat being thumped down on the wooden table at the end of the counter which she had seen in a flash as she tore into the shop. Next he sharpened a knife. 'If he finds me he'll kill me,' thought Pansy wildly. No, he wouldn't, of course he wouldn't! After the knife he did some chopping and sawing. Then a customer came in. He said, 'Good afternoon, Madam.'

'Good afternoon, Butcher. That steak you sent me was practically uneatable. It was abominably tough although Cook beat it for half an hour,' said the customer crossly.

'Tough? I can't understand that, Madam. It was the best, the very best. I wouldn't dream of sending you anything but the best, you know that, Madam.'

'I should like to think so, but if you give me any further

cause for complaint I shall have no choice but to transfer my custom elsewhere. And now, I want a small sirloin sent round immediately, please.'

The butcher promised to do that; he had exactly what she wanted, he said. He was most humble and apologetic again about the steak. While he was seeing Madam out of the door, Pansy managed to get her face a little further away from the tin of nastiness. When he came back he was muttering angrily to himself, 'Complaining old so-and-so; I'll give 'er tough steak one of these days.'

Oh dear, Pansy did wish he hadn't been put in a bad temper in case he found her. If only he would go away again. But he did some more chopping and sawing and knifing – the silent times were the knifing ones she thought – and then, passing her again, she heard him open a door and bellow, 'George! Come on up, George!'

The butcher was back at the table by the time George came. He came so quietly Pansy didn't hear him till suddenly his feet were there. He had on brown sandshoes; there was a hole in one and his big toe was sticking through, and the nail was long and black. The bottoms of his grey flannel trousers came to just above his ankles.

'George, take this sirloin to 20 Grosvenor Terrace and don't make a mistake, mind, or we won't 'ave 'er orders no more, and I've never known a 'ousehold eat meat so 'earty as they eats it – you'd think they was a pack of bloomin' wolves. And while you're at it, drop some offal in for the Red Lion cats –' The butcher's boots came close up to Pansy. Then his hand came under the counter and grabbed the tin.

He had seen her. The tin clattered back onto the floor and nearly but didn't quite, upset. 'What the devil! Come on, out of that!' Grabbing Pansy's shoulder, the butcher pulled her out. 'Ah – it's one of those limbs from the Poor-house – what are you up to, skulking there? Out with it!'

The butcher's cheeks were meaty, with little red veins; they had a raw look. He had a brown moustache waxed into points. His hair was smarmed slantways across his forehead as though it were glued there.

'I'm not from the Workhouse really,' Pansy began, but before she could explain any more he interrupted.

'I know what they wears up there all right and you're one of 'em, and if you aren't stealing' – thrusting his fingers into the pocket of Leah's frock; they came out with a cockleshell – 'then you're running away and that don't do neither. George, take 'er down and lock 'er in and I'll 'ave to take her back after closing. I'm not getting the wrong side of the law nor 'elping no one else to get there neither.'

'No! Please let me explain!' cried Pansy, struggling, but the butcher's grip was like a vice.

'Now don't start creating, it ain't a mite o' good, and don't you stand there like a dolt, George; do what you're told, take 'er and 'op it – there's that old windbag from the Fox and Goose coming.'

George seemed as strong as the butcher although he was only a big boy. Pansy fought the whole way – to the door through which George had come, and then down the stone steps, which were almost dark when the butcher had slammed shut the door behind them. The boy shoved her through another, open, door at the bottom and then, shutting it, stood against it. They were in a small room hung with meat.

'I don't belong to the Workhouse,' Pansy cried. 'He can't take me there.'

'Wotcher doin' in them togs if yer don't b'long?' George demanded. 'T'ain't reason.'

Pansy had had a look at his face which was rather spotty. 'Listen –'

When she had explained everything he said, 'They can't murder yer if ole Green takes yer back.'

'They might not kill me,' Pansy agreed, 'there'd be talk if they did, but I think they'd be dreadful, most dreadfully beastly; they'd put me in the cupboard and beat me too, I dare say.'

' 'E'll take yer even if yer don't b'long. Once 'e's made up 'is mind 'e's that pig'eaded there's no a'budgin' of 'im.'

'Please let me out,' Pansy pleaded.

'Not with 'im in the shop I can't.'

65

'George!' the butcher's voice came bellowing.

'I gotter go but I'll come back. Keep a stout 'eart,' said George kindly, 'an' don't make no bloomin' row; 'e can't 'arf turn nasty when 'e's roused.'

Pansy found it impossible to keep a stout heart when George slammed and bolted the door; it was all she could do not to batter on it and screech. It was almost as bad as the cupboard, she thought wildly; it was bigger though, being a room, and there was a dirty window at the top of one wall which, although it was out of reach and she could only see bricks through it, made her feel less shut in than she would have in a cupboard. But she *was* shut in. 'When you are anxious and there is nothing you can do but wait, try to occupy your mind with something pleasant,' Aunt Susu had said when Ginie had gone to the dentist. The dentist would be better than this, Pansy thought. She tried to occupy her mind with the carcasses hanging round the walls; there was a string of sausages too, but they weren't particularly pleasant, and she stopped. She was still among strangers – not the carcasses, they didn't count, but George and the butcher did. She must rely on her own resources – though she didn't see how she could manage without George and extricate herself again.

There was an empty tin; turning it upside down she sat on it to think. If she escaped – and she didn't see how she

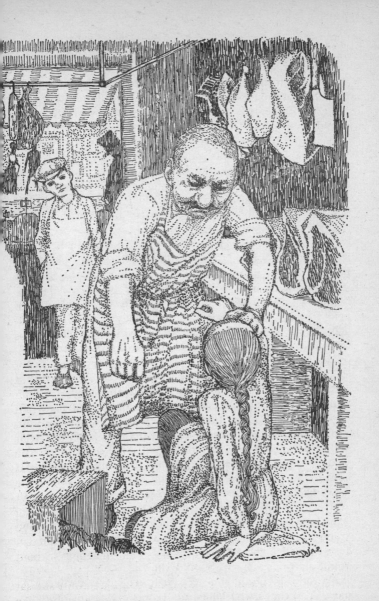

could unless George helped her which she hoped and hoped he would – it would probably be too late to find Nonna at the harbour, unless he came back almost at once. She would go straight to the station and Leah would have to go back to the Workhouse in her clothes. She couldn't bear the thought of the awfulness of what Long Nose and Matron would do to her. 'And it's my fault,' Pansy thought miserably, 'but if I did go I don't think I could save her.' Even if she was able to, she was too afraid to go back to them on the beach, or to the Workhouse if they had gone there. At the thought of it her whole inside seemed to tremble. It wouldn't be so dreadful if she could go with Atalanta or Nonna. They would do something to help Leah if they could, Pansy knew.

Shutting her eyes, Pansy tried to see Nonna in her blue frock and grass hat talking to Long Nose and Matron in her trailing way; she could see Nonna, but she couldn't see what *they'd* be like. Would Long Nose behave as though Nonna wasn't there till she had finished and then turn on her? If only Grandfather was here! He would be the most help. If she wrote a letter tomorrow which was Sunday it wouldn't get to him till Monday, and although he might rescue Leah and make the Workhouse a better place, Leah would have had an awful time by then.

Pansy turned her thoughts from Leah's plight to her own. If Nonna and Atalanta weren't at the station, what should she do? She hadn't any money; her treat and donkey money was in the pocket of her own frock, she had just remembered. She couldn't buy a ticket without any money, and if they weren't catching the train she wouldn't want to. Suppose the train had gone when she got there and she didn't know if they were on it? 'I'll have to walk.' It was twelve miles; Mr Chubb had told them. Even if George came soon – and he did mean to help her, she was sure – she would have to walk a lot of the way in the dark – or sleep under a hedge the way tramps did. No, she wouldn't, she would sleep in a stack. Should she burrow into the straw like a rat? Or should she sleep with her face out under the stars? Yes, that's what she'd do. It was a pleasant thought, much pleasanter than the carcasses, and she felt immensely cheered for a bit, till she thought again: suppose George didn't come? She would have to run away from the butcher, then, on the way to the Workhouse. It was a pity she looked as if she belonged there. If everyone tried to catch her and take her back it was going to be very dangerous indeed, as bad as being a spy – worse. Spies looked like everyday kind of people whom even their friends wouldn't suspect; but everyone would suspect her. Fancy having a more dangerous time than a spy! A little spurt of pride went through her. But spies were shot if they were caught. 'They can't shoot me,' Pansy said to the nearest carcass.

Somewhere a clock struck five. The train was starting in five minutes. Pansy saw it with her mind's eye, and she saw Nonna and Atalanta staring out of the window waiting for her to come – or would they? She stopped seeing Nonna at the window and saw her sitting in the corner instead. For a second she saw Atalanta sitting reading *The Wide Wide World* – but she wouldn't, surely? Surely she'd look? Would they worry?

Pansy was not sure they would, not like the Aunts and Nana. The thought of their going made her feel dreadfully alone and abandoned. She wanted again to beat the door and scream. She mustn't. She said the alphabet backwards instead, 'ZYX and WV,UTS and RQP,ON –' Before she had time to say 'M' she heard feet on the stairs. 'The butcher!' she thought wildly.

The key turned, the door opened, it was George.

Pansy, who had jumped up from the tin, said, 'Oh, I *am* glad it's you!'

' 'Old the door open I gotter get the steps through.'

When he had pulled them in, making rather a noise so that Pansy was afraid the butcher would hear, she shut the door politely behind him as though she didn't want to escape, and asked excitedly, 'Am I going through the window? Where's the butcher? Didn't he hear you coming?'

'No, you ain't goin' through the winder.' Putting the steps by the wall, George went up them and opened it.

'But I am, I must be,' said Pansy in amazement.

'No, you ain't, you're going outer the door. Shop's shut, ole Green's gone to get 'is paper whiles I starts clearin' up. When 'e finds yer gone 'e'll think you've made off through the winder. These steps are mostly kept down 'ere and if 'e ain't seed them in the yard he's notter know they wasn't 'ere an' I bringed 'em down, see?'

Yes, Pansy saw. What a gorgeous plan! She felt a little disappointed that she wasn't going through the window, but she didn't argue, naturally. 'Will he be cross with you for having the steps down there so that I could get out? He won't beat you, will he?' she asked anxiously.

Beat me – I'd like to see 'im try! 'E won't 'arf give me a piece of 'is mind though, but e'll be glad too, I reckons. 'E won't 'ave ter trouble ter take yer up ter the Poor-house an' 'e won't 'ave done nothin' 'gainst law in not takin' yer seein' as you's not there ter take.' Opening the door, George listened. 'Now c'mon an' see 'ere – don't go runnin', walk proper, as if yer knows where you's goin' and there's no 'arm in goin' there neither. Don't look s'picious.'

'I'll try not to,' Pansy promised, 'but I had to run before; I was being chased.'

'Where you goin'?'

'Home,' said Pansy, 'at least it isn't *home* but where I'm staying. I've missed the train and I'll have to walk. It's twelve miles along the cliff, Mr Chubb said, and fifteen by road because it winds, and about seven as the crow flies and he reckoned the train was shorter than the road and the cliff and longer than the crow.'

George scratched his head, 'Well it ain't far anyway.'

'No, I shall do the twelve miles along the cliff,' said Pansy, trying to sound as if twelve miles was nothing. She had never walked twelve miles before, but with a sleep in a stack in the middle it wouldn't be twelve in one day. She was just going to mention her sleeping plans when George told her to 'C'mon, 'op it.'

'I don't want to go to the beach,' she whispered as they went up the stairs. 'Can I get to the cliff without going there?' She felt she had to whisper although George didn't seem to be creeping exactly.

70

'Easy,' he said quite loudly when he reached the door at the top. 'Up the street' – jerking his head to the right – 'turn right at the Fox and Goose then straight on till you's out o'town and there y'are.' Taking a newspaper from a pile on the counter, he thrust it at Pansy. 'Take this.'

Pansy grabbed it obediently. 'Why?'

'Yer can sleep under it 'appen yer don't get there afore night an' if someone eyes yer, yer can open it up an' read, see. I knows 'cos I've run away meself.'

'Have you!' cried Pansy forgetting the butcher and everything else at this exciting news. 'Oh, how gorgeous! Why did you run?'

'I ain't tellin' yer now. If yer mucks about any longer 'e'll be back an' catch yer. 'Op it.'

'Yes,' said Pansy with sudden fright. 'Thank you for saving me, thank you very much indeed, I –' she wanted to say she'd like to do something for him.

'Go on.'

'Good-bye,' Pansy went. She walked very quickly without running although she wanted to run dreadfully. She didn't look back till she reached the Fox and Goose. There was no sign of George or the butcher.

8

SUPPER LOST AND SUPPER FOUND

THE street led out nearly to the end of the parade. Right at
the end the cliffs started. The beach was empty here except
for two fishing boats and some lobster-pots and some nets
spread on the shingle to dry. There was a fisherman bent
double in one of the boats which suited Pansy better than if
he had been standing up staring. She gazed back along the
beach, but the crowded part where the people and tents and
pier were was too far away for her to pick out any Workhouse children or anyone else. She felt much safer so near
the cliff. She did wish she had got some food, though. There
was a little shop with a bow-window facing the sea in
the last of the buildings. She went to have a quick look
to see what she could have bought if she had had some
money.

There was a bit of all sorts – buckets and spades and balls
and pink peppermint rock and buns and toffee-apples and
pasties and pork pies. The minute Pansy saw the pork pies
she wanted one so much she could hardly bear it. They
were dangerous in hot weather, that's why they never had
them at home, and this was very hot weather. The thought
that it might be bad made her feel a little better. She was
just going away when a voice behind her startled her.
'Want something to eat, kid?'

Why had she stayed to look? Feeling very afraid again,
Pansy turned. It was a fat boy of about fifteen in a striped
blazer with a school cap on the back of his head. Before she
had decided what to say, he took a coin out of his pocket
and handed it to her. 'Here's sixpence – get yourself some
grub with it. There's some jolly decent looking pork pies

there – get one of them, and what about an orange if they've got some, and a bar of choc.'

How very kind he was. 'Thanks awfully,' said Pansy shyly.

'That's all right. Go on –' he gave her a little shove towards the door, and strolled off, whistling.

The bell jangled loudly when Pansy opened the door. The shop was empty. While she waited for someone to come – and she wanted them to come quickly so that she could escape up on to the cliffs – she suddenly thought what she must do; she must talk like Leah. It was no good explaining she didn't belong to the Workhouse, and as she wasn't hiding under the counter and had got sixpence why should anyone think she was running away? She could pretend she had been asked out to tea if anyone became suspicious. Why shouldn't a friend of her grandfather's ask her out for a treat?

A woman came. She was short and fat with rosy cheeks and a kind face. Pansy felt immensely relieved. 'Can I 'ave one of them pork pies, please?' she said, feeling very proud of how she sounded.

''Course you may, dearie.' Bringing a bag, the woman went over to the window.

As Pansy saw the pie in her hand, she suddenly felt very uneasy. 'Is it fresh?'

'Fresh? Lawk-a-mussy, of course it's fresh, child – fresh as a daisy and no mistake!' She was staring at Pansy rather hard. 'You don't get fresh stuff up there, you poor little mite, is that it? You come from the Poorhouse, don't you, lovey?'

Pansy ducked her head. She pretended to herself she was rubbing her chin which had a tickle on it, but she knew really she was acting a lie.

'How comes it you're shopping alone? You're out with a friend p'raps?'

'Yus,' said Pansy and it was true; she was out with Nonna and Atalanta. She was pleased she had remembered to say 'yus', and pleased that the woman should think what she had wanted her to of her own accord. The 'yus' made her want to giggle for a moment, and then she was afraid. Suppose the woman was only pretending to be kind, like Long Nose? Suppose she suddenly roared at her and pounced?

'And this friend's given you some money I shouldn't wonder, and told you to get something you want and you want a pie. What else d'you fancy, ducks?' The woman looked at Pansy kindly, not away as Long Nose had. Of course there was no one else there, like Matron, for her to look at and talk to. But her face was nice.

Pansy took heart again. 'A bottle of lemonade, please.' She was dreadfully thirsty, she wanted it much more than an orange. 'It's fourpence, ain't it – and the pie tuppence? I've got sixpence.'

'That's right, then you're all fair and square. Wouldn't wonder if you'd like a bun – a nice Chelsea.' The woman put one in the bag with the pork pie and picked up a stick of pink rock. 'You don't have no rock up there I reckon.' Then she took a bottle of lemonade, and next she unhitched a string bag from a nail. 'Here's a bag for it. It had some balls in it but I sold the last this morning, and it'll do nicely to carry the lot.'

'I've only got sixpence,' said Pansy, putting the coin on the counter.

'That's right, but no one's going to say Marge Parsons's a skinflint when charity's knocking at her door.' Picking up the coin, she stared at it. 'This isn't sixpence. It's a foreign coin by the looks of it.' She looked at Pansy rather hard again, but for another reason now. 'Did you know?'

'No,' Pansy said, and began to get scarlet with embarrassment so that she knew she was looking as though she had known. 'I thought it was sixpence; he said it was.'

'Who? Where did you get it from?'

'A boy gave it to me outside. He saw me looking in the window and told me to get some grub with it.' She had forgotten to speak like Leah although *grub* sounded a bit like what she might have said. They weren't allowed to say 'grub' at home.

'Having you on, the little blighter! Lucky for you, Marge Parsons has got a kind heart under here' – she patted her blue blouse – 'so you'll get your things all the same, dearie, money or no money.'

Pansy thanked her very much. She remembered that she wanted to talk like Leah, but she didn't see how you could say 'Thank you very much,' differently.

'What comes you're up there?' Marge Parsons was staring hard again for the other reason now. 'You don't seem quite as if you should be.'

Just then the bell jangled and a lady came into the shop with a pug. Pansy would have loved to scrutinize the pug, but she had no more time for that than she had had for the bulldog. Relieved at the diversion, she said 'Good morning' politely, and hurried out.

Outside, with her bag of food, Pansy felt happy and excited. She would have a picnic on the cliffs. She walked gaily and fast as though she knew where she was going, which she did. Suddenly, she heard steps behind her and glancing round anxiously, saw it was the boy.

'Hullo,' he said, 'you seem to have got a dashed lot for sixpence. Give it to me; I'll carry it for you.'

'No, it's all right,' said Pansy. 'She gave it to me. It wasn't sixpence, it was a foreign coin.'

'What if it was? She can pass it on, can't she?' Laughing, he made a grab at the bag. 'Come on, sucker!'

Wrenching free, Pansy began to run, but before she had got under way, the boy's boot tripped her up and she fell headlong. Snatching the bag, he went off with it.

Picking herself up, Pansy began to cry. Her knees hurt dreadfully and one of her hands. Looking round, hardly knowing that she did, she saw the boy with the bag jump off the parade on to the shingle. 'Beast!' She went on towards the cliff. She had no hanky; Leah hadn't had one. Wiping her eyes with her frock, she tried to stop crying. Up on the cliff she could cry as loudly and as long as she liked; not now.

A Bath chair came along drawn by a donkey. The old lady in the chair looked a beak-nosed old cross-patch. She put up a lorgnette to stare at Pansy. 'Isn't that one of the Workhouse children?' she shouted. 'They seem to be allowed to run wild these days. When the General was on the Governing Committee they were kept under control.' Her dumpy little companion walking beside the chair in a violet toque, had smiled at Pansy, but Pansy was out of earshot when she answered. Disobeying George, she had started to run.

In spite of her knees and hand, she ran right on to the end of the parade and then started clambering up the grassy slope. Her breath was coming in sobbing puffs. She stopped for a moment and then puffed on. At the top she stopped and looked all ways. She could see the cliffs for a long way and there was no one coming. She looked down the way she had come and there was no one coming up after her. Where the grass stretched away till it came to a field on the left there was no sign of anyone either, and the great stretch of sea was empty too except for one small black ship on the horizon. She was alone. She could cry as long and loudly as she liked, but now she could she didn't want to any more. Her eyes watered a bit as she examined her injuries, that was all.

Her hand was scraped but wasn't bleeding. Her right knee was; there was a large hole in Leah's stocking, and blood. Taking off the garter, she rolled down the stocking to her ankle. The lovely coolness of her bare leg was a tremendous relief. The bleeding had stopped but her knee was raw. She had nothing, not even a hanky, to bind it up with. Her other knee wasn't nearly so bad. As she rolled down the stocking and rolled up her sleeves, she thought about her pork pie and the lemonade; those were what she really minded about, more than her injuries and more than the Chelsea bun and the rock. She was so frightfully thirsty and she had been longing to eat the pork pie. There was nothing to have a picnic with now; she had got to go hungry and thirsty for twelve miles. Grandfather had a patient who ate too much and walked too little; now she was going to eat too little and walk too much. She had missed tea already. If she missed supper and breakfast she would be three meals behind. If she was back at the farm in time for dinner tomorrow she would have to eat three times as much

76

of everything to make up; she would have to eat nine potatoes. Pansy laughed; her laugh floated up just as a swooping gull screeched.

Where the sea sparkled the sun beat down into it like golden raindrops. Away from the sparkle it was the colour of her blue watered-silk party sash. She didn't want her party frock on now, naturally, but how she longed for her own cotton one. She had never hated a frock so much as this of Leah's.

She walked for quite a long time before she saw anyone: Then she suddenly came upon him, a small old man sitting near a gorse bush beside the path. He had on rusty-black trousers and a rusty-black coat and nothing on his chest which was pink. Beside him lay a flat white thing on the grass. Pansy, who would have liked to ask the time, looked at the view instead. She didn't think he would want her to see him sunning his chest. When she had passed him she bent down and, pretending to do up the lace of her boot, looked back at him. He was putting on the white thing which turned out to be a shirt-front. This surprised her a good deal and it made it easier to ask the time. Turning round, she went the little way back. 'Good afternoon,' she said politely. 'Could you tell me what time it is, please?'

'Most certainly.' From the breast pocket of his coat, he took a large turnip watch on the end of a chain fastened through his buttonhole. 'Thirty-two minutes and four seconds past the hour of five o'clock,' he said in a high cultured voice. Pansy knew a high cultured voice when she heard one because Miss Darcey, who made necklaces with beads of wallpaper for missionary bazaars, had one; Aunt Susu said so. 'In the year of our Lord nineteen-hundred and eleven,' he continued as if Pansy didn't know which year she was alive in.

'I knew it was nineteen-hundred and eleven.'

'You may, but a savage wouldn't.'

'Did you think I was a savage?'

Putting away his watch, he scrutinized her speculatively with small bright eyes like a bird. 'Who can say? Appearances are sometimes exceedingly deceptive.'

'But you must know I don't come from a desert island, or the jungle or anywhere like that. I may have rather a funny frock on and my stockings and boots aren't what they might be, but I *have* got things on,' Pansy pointed out, 'and I'm not a cannibal.'

'Neither are a multitude of savages – white ones. Oh, yes, there are plenty of white savages; they don't live in the jungle, they are to be seen in carriages, quite often in fine expensive clothes.'

'You mean they can behave like savages whoever they are? But if they wear clothes and aren't cannibals and don't live in the jungle,' said Pansy slowly, 'what do they do that's savage?'

'It's not so much what they do as what they don't do – their profound ignorance. The older you grow the more you will find that the ignorance of man is quite extraordinary.'

'Do you think I shall?' asked Pansy doubtfully.

'They've all got bodies,' he went on as though she hadn't spoken, 'but they don't know the simplest things about them. They'll oil their bicycles, manure their tomatoes, protect their furs with moth-balls, syringe their roses to kill the blight, but when it comes to their own bodies and the cure for their ailments, they haven't the knowledge of an animal.' Pulling a haversack towards him, he opened the flap and pulled out a blue flower. 'Do you know what this is?'

Yes, Pansy did. 'Viper's bugloss,' she said proudly. She knew a lot of wild flowers now from her walks with Grandfather.

'Exactly. Do you know its medicinal properties?'

'No,' admitted Pansy reluctantly. She didn't know what *medicinal properties* were as a matter of fact, so she had to say 'no' if she didn't ask and she didn't want to.

'Of course you don't; you're as bad as the rest of them. You wouldn't dream of making a tisane with its leaves if you had a headache.'

'What's a tisane?' Cross at being lumped with the savages, she didn't care now if he did think her ignorant.

He clicked his tongue, 'Never heard of decoction?'

'*Con*coction,' Pansy corrected him triumphantly. 'It's something mixed up with something else.'

'Decoction is what I said; a decoction is the liquid formed by the boiling down of something. The decoction formed by the boiling down of the leaves of the viper's bugloss will relieve your headache.'

'I haven't got one,' Pansy said, 'but Nana has them and when I get home I'll get some viper's bugloss – I know where it grows, there's some by the downs track – and make a decoction ready.' She felt so excited by the prospect she could scarcely wait.

'How? You don't know, and when you've made it you don't know how much to drink. It's quite simple: pour a pint of boiling water on an ounce of leaves, leave it to infuse for twenty minutes, and drink it in a teacup.' Delving into the haversack again, he produced a scarlet pimpernel.

Pansy, who had just said 'Thank you' for the viper's bugloss recipe, said 'Scarlet pimpernel' in a rush before he could.

'Naturally. Do you know what the Greeks used it for? Diseases of the eye. It can also remove freckles.'

'*Freckles?*' said Pansy, astonished. 'Leah –' She stopped; he didn't know anything about Leah.

'Dispels melancholic and relieves rheumatism.'

'How can it do all that?'

'How can the juice of knotgrass cure nose-bleeding, and camomile hysteria, and mullein coughs and colds? Because the Almighty intended that they should. The herbs of the field have their uses just as the birds of the air and the fishes of the sea, and all animals great and small have theirs. What, may I ask, has scraped your knee? Stone by the look of it.'

'The parade scraped it.' Pansy thought this rather funny, but she didn't laugh; she was trying not to laugh at jokes to be like Atalanta. 'A beastly boy tripped me up and took away my food.' Her voice quivered suddenly with misery, which she hadn't known it was going to.

'Violence actuated by greed – a horrible disease and very prevalent. It attacks nations as well as individuals.'

It sounded important like that, but the boy was beastly not ill, thought Pansy rather put out. She related what had happened.

'If he is fat and does violence to obtain food, you can bet your boots he is a perennial over-feeder and a third of a pint of an infusion of clivers should be taken three times a day.'

They were not her boots, Pansy nearly said and then stopped. She didn't think he knew her clothes were Workhouse clothes and she decided not to tell him in case he was like the butcher. Not that he could catch her naturally; she could run much faster than this little old man.

Reaching for a black bag from behind him, he opened it with a click. It was a Gladstone bag. Grandfather had one and Pansy knew all about them; they were called after Mr Gladstone who had been Prime Minister in the reign of Queen Victoria and had always used one. Taking out a little pot from the bag and unscrewing the top, he held it out to Pansy. 'Anoint your wounds with that, but first be seated.'

Thanking him, Pansy took the pot and sat down which she was glad to do; she needed a rest. She did hope the stuff wasn't going to sting. Her knee was so dreadfully sore she couldn't bear to touch it, but she would have to. Taking a little of the ointment, she smeared it on gingerly.

'More, take more as if you were buttering bread extravagantly,' he ordered.

'What is it?' asked Pansy who found it cool and soothing.

'Green oil of Charity – an unguent compiled from adder's tongue and hog's fat.'

'Hog's fat!'

Ignoring hog's fat, he brought out a bulging green silk handkerchief from the bag. Unknotting it, he laid out some bread and cheese and a large yellow William pear with spots on it. 'Would you care to share my repast?' he invited in his high cultured voice.

Pansy would. She knew she ought to ask if he could spare it, but she was too hungry to suggest he couldn't. Besides, you must never look a gift-horse in the mouth. With her mind's eye she saw a horse with its mouth wide open, a white paper parcel tied with blue ribbon between its yellow teeth. She did wish he had got some drink.

Taking a knife out of his pocket, he opened it, and cut a doorstep of bread and a slice of cheese. Handing them to Pansy, he picked up the pear.

'I don't need any pear, thank you,' she said. She did, she needed it very much indeed. She was so parched with thirst that, although she was so hungry too, she wasn't sure that she could manage all that bread without it; but in spite of thirst and the gift-horse, she had to offer to let him eat it all himself, 'You have that, please.' She did hope he would know she was only being polite.

He seemed to. 'Take what you're given and be thankful.' Cutting the pear down from calyx to stem, he gave her half.

'I am thankful, I only thought –'

'Don't think.'

When they had finished eating, he brought out a bottle of brown stuff. Pansy knew it at once for what it was – cold tea. Russell, the Close gardener, always brought it to work with him. Uncorking the bottle, he handed it to her. The cheese had been so strong and the bread so stale, she was thirstier than ever, so that although it looked rather disgusting, she was delighted to accept. 'How much shall I drink?'

'Half.'

'Will you tell me if I'm going too far, please?'

'Common sense will tell you.'

She was so thirsty she wasn't sure that it would, but as a matter of fact a little seemed to go a long way; it was such a gurgling business and it was difficult not to spit. When she handed it back she hadn't got half-way.

He did not gurgle at all. Throwing back his head, he poured it down like water down a drain.

When everything was over and the bottle and handkerchief and knife had been put away, Pansy said she was afraid she must go.

'Have you far to walk?'

If she said twelve miles he might think it so far he would ask awkward questions, she thought. She said, 'Along the cliff a bit.'

'When I was your age I thought nothing of walking twenty miles.'

Pansy's twelve seemed to dwindle into nothingness; she was glad she hadn't mentioned it.

'People seem to forget they've got feet on the end of their legs. Well, you'd better be getting along.'

He wanted her to go, Pansy thought, and she thought she knew why. He wanted to take off his starched front again and sun his chest. It was still boiling hot. Saying good-bye, she went on her way.

9

ATALANTA AND LEAH

THE next interesting thing that Pansy came to was a tandem lying on the ground. Grandfather had a bicycle and Canon Andrews a tricycle, but although she had seen one at a distance she had never been at close quarters with a tandem before. She would have liked to have had a good stare, but the two people who had been on the two empty seats were somewhere, and Grandfather had said that a good spy was never careless however safe he thought he was, and although she wasn't a spy, she mustn't be careless either. And then Pansy thought the most awful thing – suppose the two people were Long Nose and Matron who had bicycled along the track to cut her off? No, she thought, no, *no*! She wanted to run, but she didn't; she walked on quietly, ready to run if she had to, her heart hammering inside her like the clapper of a bell.

They were lying on the other side of a hummock. The man was lying on his back with his head under a newspaper. He wasn't Long Nose. He had on brown knickerbockers and a white shirt and was rather fat. His thick hairy legs went down into white woollen socks rolled round his ankles like Leah's stockings round Pansy's. His shoes were brown canvas. And his companion wasn't Matron; she had a tight red frock with big white daisies all over it, and a lot of fair hair like a pile of hay. Her white shoes lay sprawling as though she had kicked them off, and the soles of her white stockings were rather dirty.

Leah's boots, with Pansy's feet in them, made so little noise on the turf they didn't hear her. But although this was a great relief she had just remembered *dogs*. She had discussed the whole business of dogs with Grandfather one day when they were picking gooseberries together. Dogs were very useful for catching escaped convicts, he had told her; they smelt them out like hounds on the trail of a fox. 'But suppose they don't smell, suppose the convicts are clean?' Pansy had asked. 'Don't they wash in prison?' Yes, washing was compulsory, Grandfather believed, although he shouldn't wonder, he had said, if some of the prisoners were as shy of water as cats. 'Frightened of it?' Pansy had been astonished. 'Unwilling to come in contact with it, shall we say. But washing is immaterial, although an unwashed person naturally smells more strongly than a washed. Everyone has his own smell however clean he is, although perhaps neither you nor I could smell it – only the dog who has a very keen nose.' He had gone on to explain how a dog would be given one of the fugitive's garments to sniff to enable it to pick up the right scent.

The dog would be given *her* frock to sniff, thought Pansy wildly, and then remembered that it would smell of Leah now as well if Leah had put it on, and Leah's would smell of her; their smells were muddled. She hoped they would muddle the dog, but she was afraid they might not. And then she remembered what Grandfather had said about water. Water broke a trail. The scent got lost in it. That was why fugitives often swam rivers if they could. She couldn't because there wasn't one, but she could get into the sea and paddle all along the edge. No, she couldn't, she couldn't get down the cliff. She would just have to go on walking on dry ground.

Pansy walked and walked. It was very inconvenient not having a watch. Atalanta would probably say she ought to be able to tell the time by the sun, but she couldn't and she'd bet Atalanta couldn't either, not really, not to say 'Now it's six' or 'Now it's seven'. She could tell it was getting late when the sun set, but so could Pansy. Just now it seemed to be taking a long time to get later. She knew what she ought to do, she ought to walk till it was nearly dark but still light enough to find a stack. If she left it till it was too dark to see one it would be simply awful.

The tireder she got the more she thought of the stack, She would have go inland to find one, a bit at any rate. She had seen one in a field just after passing the people with the tandem, but it had been much too early to stop of course, and she hadn't seen another since, or any people, or any dogs either. 'They may cut me off when I'm least expecting it,' she thought. She would be in great jeopardy if anyone came now. She was too tired to run very fast and Leah's right boot had begun to hurt.

The sea was getting less sunny. Pansy had never longed to go to bed so much before – to stack, not bed! Laughing – the laugh sounded rather odd in the solitude – she flopped down for a moment to rest. Lying back, she put her head on a tussock soft with the roots of sea-pinks. If the dogs came now she wouldn't have a dog's chance. How frightfully funny! She did *wish* she could say that to Atalanta. But it was true, which wasn't funny at all really. She felt frightened lying on her back like that. She sat up. The cliff was empty. That was how she wanted it, but it was lonely. Getting up, she started to plod on again, limping a little because of her right foot.

Quite soon she came to where a path led out from between two fields. She could go up that and find a stack. She was just turning to go when someone spoke.

'Talk about snails, what on *earth* have you been doing?'

Pansy's heart jumped. Looking round wildly, she saw Atalanta sitting on a molehill by a gorse bush reading *The Wide Wide World*. The relief was tremendous; she gave a little gasp of delight as the fear oozed out of her. 'How did you get here?' she asked eagerly.

'Walked,' said Atalanta.

'But you hate walking,' said Pansy, amazed.

'I hate school and tennis and tapioca, but they are forced upon me.'

'Did you come along the cliff?' Pansy asked.

'Of course I did.'

'But you walk so slowly; why didn't I catch you up?' Pansy sank down on the grass. 'When did you start?'

'When I missed the train.' Atalanta clapped a mosquito to death on her leg. It was all over quite quickly, and she was back again as she had been, looking still and sleepy.

'Then you had a good start,' Pansy told her. "I was still shut up with the meat then.'

Atalanta didn't say *'Meat?'* She did not seem in the least surprised that Pansy had been shut up with it. She didn't say anything. She simply turned over a page of *The Wide Wide World.*

'Where's Nonna? What's happened to Leah?' Pansy asked.

'Nonna's in the Rectory or was, and Leah's in the cupboard now, I expect – unless she's been and come out again,' said Atalanta.

'Oh, I did hope someone would stop it happening!' Pulling a blade of grass, Pansy thrust it into her mouth and bit furiously.

'That's what Nonna's gone to the Rectory to do. The Church may step in where a Governing Body has failed.'

Pansy said nothing for a moment; she was too impressed. Then she asked Atalanta, 'Did you make that up or did Nonna say it?'

'Don't be silly; I'm saying it. It means that the Rector may be able to stop Leah being put in the cupboard or get her out of it if she's in there, whereas the committee of Governors who are top dogs over Long Nose don't know about the cupboard at all, at least they may know it's there but they don't know what goes on in it – unless they're conniving.'

'Conniving?'

'Agreeing to let the Workhouse children be shut up in it,' Atalanta explained, 'but I shouldn't think they are. I expect they're just plumb ignorant.'

Pansy quite saw how plumb ignorant the committee of Governors must be if they didn't know what went on in the cupboard, but that was better than conniving. 'Someone ought to tell them!' she burst out. 'Nonna or the Rector.'

'I expect they will, but' – Atalanta yawned – 'they'll have to wait for a committee meeting to tell the whole lot in a

bunch which is best. You and I ought to do that. If the Chairman's got any sense he'll ask us to.'

'Would Long Nose and Matron be there?' Pansy asked. The thought of seeing them again, even with other people, terrified her.

'I hope so,' said Atalanta, 'listening to some home truths.'

How brave Atalanta was, thought Pansy. But she stopped seeing the committee meeting with her mind's eye, seeing Long Nose wanting to murder her while she said how awful he was as she would have to do, and she went back to seeing Leah in the cupboard instead. 'It's our fault if Leah's in the cupboard. If you'd never suggested changing clothes and I hadn't *urged* her to, she'd never have bathed and she'd have been all right.'

'And she would have missed the biggest bit of fun she's had for ages,' Atalanta said.

This warmed Pansy's heart and she felt greatly comforted. 'Tell me what happened and then I'll tell you.'

Sighing, Atalanta laid *The Wide Wide World* open on the grass beside her, and thrusting her hand through her fringe, looked as though she were trying to wake up. She began at the point when she and Leah were still in the sea. Atalanta without her specs hadn't of course seen Matron come up to Pansy and box her ears, but Leah, watching sharp-eyed, had told her what was happening. 'She's boxed 'er ears; comed up be'ind an' did it sudden.' Atalanta had thought this extremely loathsome and had said so, but it was nothing new to Leah. 'Box, box – er's for ever boxin'.'

'Well she ought to be ashamed of herself. Doesn't she know it can injure the ear drums?' Atalanta had said.

'Wot's they?'

'Drums in your ears, of course – the things you hear with,' Atalanta had explained. 'What's happening now?' she had asked. When Leah had said. 'She's on at 'er,' Atalanta had said they must go in and started to wade towards the shore.

'I can't never go!' Leah wailed.

'You can't stay in the sea for the rest of your life,' Atalanta had pointed out.

'I'd rather drown, sure I would.'

'You can't do that either, it's too shallow. Come on and don't be a coward.' It had taken ages to wade in, and while they were doing it, Leah reported what was happening on the beach and talked of cupboards and murder and starvation.

'Stop crying,' Atalanta had ordered. 'They can't murder you as I've already told you; they'd be hanged if they did and it wouldn't be worth it. They're obviously bullies both of them, and if you go on snivelling they'll be worse. You've got to stand up to them. I'll help you. We've got to make them see that bathing isn't a crime – not a heinous one at any rate, even if it *is* forbidden. I shall speak to them firmly.'

'Aw, miss, 'ow can you! You aren't 'arf brave!'

No, Atalanta had said, she wasn't brave. Brave people were people who did things although they were frightened and she wasn't frightened.

'They can't kill *you*; you ain't nothin' to do with 'em,' Leah wailed.

'Oh, do stop talking about killing,' Atalanta told her, 'and tell me what's happening now.'

'Matron's got 'er an's a'draggin' of 'er up the beach to Long Nose, that's where er's a'takin' of 'er, I'll wager.'

'Yes, I expect it is,' Atalanta agreed.

When they had reached the wet sand at the edge of the sea, Leah exclaimed, ' 'Er's runnin' away, miss, and there's a boy – 'Erb, it's 'Erb – a'runnin' after 'er!' Leah had forgotten some of her fear for a moment to gape. 'Willie! – 'E's a'runnin' too.'

'Are Matron and Long Nose running?' Atalanta had inquired.

No, according to Leah, they weren't.

Pansy ought to have stuck her ground, Atalanta said. She was better at running than most things though, and Atalanta had bet she wouldn't be caught. 'We'll get dressed before we do anything,' she had told Leah.

Matron had met them on their way to the tent. She had been absolutely furious in a vicious beastly way. Grabbing Leah's arms she had said they were both coming straight up to the Master. 'I'm not, I'm going to dress,' Atalanta had told her. 'You can't bully me and if you try I'll make a scene in front of the whole beach and have you up for assault.' She had won. But Matron had come with them to the tent; she had come inside, if you could call that winning, and the moment they arrived she had let go of Leah's arm where the marks of her fingers showed red and purple and boxed her ears. 'Take that, you deceitful little devil!'

There had been a frightful row between Matron and Atalanta. 'She said she would have the law on us,' Atalanta told Pansy. 'I told her not to be silly, that I'd done nothing at all, that it was all your fault, you'd been bossy and interfering and made Leah change clothes and bathe when she hadn't wanted to.'

'How could you be so *beastly*?' Pansy burst out. 'How could you blame me for everything when I wasn't there and when you'd suggested changing? I never sneaked about you to Matron; I pretended I'd suggested it!'

'Because you weren't there of course. How dense you are,' said Atalanta. "If you had been and I'd said it, she'd probably have given you such a clip she'd have ruptured your ear-drums for good and all. I didn't see why mine should be ruptured,' Atalanta made an unsuccessful grab at a mosquito, 'and I thought I'd try and save Leah's, if they hadn't been done in already. I said you'd only borrowed the clothes and would naturally return them, and until you had, you'd got the worst of the bargain. The woman was still in a towering rage and I could see that nothing I said was going to help Leah much, that she was going to give her hell, not to mention Long Nose. Those two need a stretch of solitary confinement followed by hard labour.'

'What's hard labour?' asked Pansy, not using her brain very much at the moment, it was so filled with pity for Leah.

'Labouring hard, of course – breaking stones and making up roads. It would do them a power of good.'

'Yes, wouldn't it!' Pansy agreed eagerly, her thoughts turning from Leah to a vision of Long Nose and Matron crushing stones to bits with hammers. No, they would use pickaxes, she expected.

'I told Matron when she said about having the law on us that she wouldn't stand a chance in court,' continued Atalanta. 'Prosecution would make mincemeat of her, and they might do more; they might *ferret* out things.'

Pansy gasped, staring at Atalanta with admiration. Then she had an idea, 'Humphrey could prosecute!' she clapped her hands. Humphrey Robertson-Fortescue was Atalanta's barrister uncle.

'He wouldn't take it on, I shouldn't think,' said Atalanta. 'Now he's so famous he prefers murders.'

'Perhaps,' Pansy said, 'they *did* murder Gertie – you know the one Leah said fell out of window. She said they'd killed her. Perhaps Long Nose or Matron did push her out.'

'Who knows? Humphrey says there are two kinds of criminals – the bludgeoning ones who don't think, and the crafty snakes who plan things. Matron and Long Nose are crafty snakes, obviously,' said Atalanta.

If Pansy hadn't been so hot she would have shivered. She agreed in a whisper. Spiders' webs lay spread on the grass-like soft filmy grey rags. There was eggs-and-bacon and blue milkwort and thyme and, where the longer grass by the track began, toad-flax and lady's bedstraw and hawk-weed. It was all so lovely here, but there was such unloveliness elsewhere. 'What did Matron say when you said what you said to her?'

'She said Long Nose would deal with me – only she called him "the Master" naturally – and that directly I was dressed I was going with her to see him. I said that most certainly I was going to see him; I should like to.'

Snatching up a grass, Pansy thrust it rapturously into her mouth, 'Was she surprised? What did she look like?'

'I didn't look,' Atalanta said. 'I was inside the bathing-dress by that time, hauling it off my head. I forgot to undo the belt and it stuck round my chest and I couldn't see a thing.'

'How *awful*!' said Pansy. 'You were in her power.'

'She didn't touch me; I don't expect she dared,' said Atalanta coolly.

'What happened when you saw Long Nose?' Pansy asked

next. 'Did he seem nice at first and then get absolutely awful? When I saw him –'

What happened when Pansy saw him poured out of her suddenly. Once she started she went straight on telling Atalanta everything – about what happened at the butcher's, and George, about the boy giving her the coin and then taking her food, her encounter and a meal with the old man, and then about the tandem and seeing the couple it belonged to – a rigmarole that finished with her sitting here on the warm turf beside the gorse with Atalanta.

Atalanta never once interrupted. She was so still and silent she might have been asleep, but Pansy knew she wasn't. Her eyelids were half closed, but if she had been asleep they would have been absolutely closed. Besides, in the middle, Atalanta suddenly blew a fly off her nose.

When Pansy stopped talking, Atalanta took off her spectacles, misted by the heat of her face, to polish them. 'That man you had food with was a herbalist,' she said.

'A herbalist?' Pansy said wonderingly.

'Someone who cures people with herbs of course. Did you have camomile tea?' Atalanta inquired.

'I don't think so.'

'You must know. Did it taste like ordinary tea or rather extraordinary?'

'Ordinary, I think,' Pansy said, 'but cold tea tastes different from hot and sucking it out of a bottle makes it a bit different again.'

Atalanta, who had finished polishing her spectacles on the hem of her frock, put them on again slowly, hitching them over her ears. 'I wonder he asked you, you look awful,' she said.

'He didn't mind,' said Pansy, and she knew it was true. He hadn't been pretending not to mind; he hadn't.

'A pity about your pork pie,' Atalanta remarked. 'I had one from the shop and it was luscious, and a Chelsea bun and a bottle of lemonade.'

'I don't believe you?' Pansy cried. Where's the bottle?'

'Here –' Atalanta lifted one up from beside her.

Pansy glared at it furiously. It was empty.

Atalanta told her she ought never to have run away from Long Nose. Now she had, in someone else's clothes, she was a thief. 'An ordinary person wouldn't have you up I don't expect,' Atalanta went on, 'but there's no knowing what a vicious brute like that man will do. If it all comes out into the open I dare say the Lamb will expel you.'

Pansy's heart sank down into Leah's stolen boots. 'I've got my own underclothes; it's only the frock and stockings and boots and sun-bonnet, and Leah's got my frock and purse with the donkey money and my hat and sand-shoes, and you said I'd only borrowed them which was true, and I have got the worst of the bargain.'

'I don't know so much about that, what a court of law would say. You've got Leah's stockings but she hasn't got any because you hadn't,' Atalanta pointed out. 'And Leah only got sand-shoes in exchange for boots.'

'New at the beginning of the term sand-shoes,' Pansy said defiantly, 'and these boots are very old I should think *and* she's got my purse and money.'

'It's just as bad to steal old boots as a bag of diamonds,' said Atalanta stolidly, ignoring the money. 'But if we can get back without being caught you can put the whole bang-shoot into a parcel and send it back at once. Tomorrow's Sunday which is a nuisance, but first thing on Monday morning. If you can do up the parcel tomorrow you can show it to the police all ready for posting if they come, that's the important thing, to get back and take off the clothes – not that you'd want to keep them on, I should think. If we play our cards properly there's no reason why we shouldn't outwit Long Nose and the police and every-one else.'

How splendid! thought Pansy excitedly. Then she re-membered. 'Dogs,' she said, 'how can we outwit the dogs if there's no water? They may send dogs to smell me out.'

'If they do, they do,' said Atalanta baldly.

10

THEY FIND A STACK

They went up the track in search of a stack. Pansy was so pleased that Atalanta meant to sleep in one and hadn't any other sleeping plans up her sleeve, that she hardly felt the boot rubbing and almost stopped feeling tired. Atalanta plodded very slowly and while she plodded more news came out of her.

Long Nose had never pretended to be nice and gentle, even for a moment, as he had with Pansy. His eyes had looked at Atalanta like a snake's. 'But I'm not a mouse and he couldn't mesmerize me,' Atalanta said. Having lived in India Pansy knew all about snakes mesmerizing their prey and she trembled inside. Long Nose had glared at her, she told Atalanta, and Atalanta said that he obviously had a lot of different ways of behaving, like an actor.

Atalanta had told him what she had told Matron: that it was all Pansy's fault and not Leah's at all, and that Pansy had only borrowed the clothes and would return them, but he had called her a 'horrible little sneak-thief'. 'He asked for our names and addresses,' Atalanta said.

'You didn't tell him, did you? We shall never be safe again, at least I won't!' Pansy's chin trembled with fear and despair.

'I gave him my London address,' said Atalanta. 'I led him to believe we were going back tonight. I said you were staying with me as your parents lived in India, which was true.'

Pansy felt enormously relieved. They would be safe now at the farm and she would be safe when she went home to the Close, but Atalanta wouldn't be safe in London – not that *she* had stolen the clothes – 'only of course I haven't stolen them,' Pansy thought, but still he would know where Atalanta lived and it wasn't a nice thought. She said so. 'S'pose he tracks you down?'

Atalanta seemed unperturbed. 'He won't; why should he? He didn't send anyone after *me* when I walked away, and if he did my father would make mincemeat of him on the spot; he's always furious if anyone interrupts him while he's writing, and he never stops.'

'But he thinks I'm with you,' Pansy pointed out.

'Well you won't be; he'll draw a blank, and no one at home knows your address so you're all right – or if Father does he wouldn't give it to him and my mother wouldn't, either. If she wasn't in bed or acting and did see Long Nose, she would think him extremely undesirable.'

Then that was all right. 'And if he doesn't know about the farm,' said Pansy, going back to the beginning, 'we can't be followed now. I needn't have worried about dogs; he'll think we're on the London train.'

'He didn't believe me,' said Atalanta. 'He didn't believe we were going back to London tonight. Leah knows where we're staying, she'll tell them.'

Pansy's heart quickened with dismay. 'She won't, she won't sneak.'

'She will if she's tortured.'

Pansy stopped in the middle of the track. She couldn't speak for a moment, what she saw was so awful. 'They wouldn't, would they?' She started to walk again because Atalanta hadn't stopped.

'There's no telling what a couple like that will do. They wouldn't behave like the Spanish Inquisition, of course,' said Atalanta placidly, 'at least I should hope not. I dare say they'll just put her into the cupboard to starve till she answers, but she won't starve to death because Nonna's blood's up. It doesn't come up often, but when it does she gets going, and she's determined to do something tonight. She hopes to catch them red-handed with the help of the Rector.'

Snatching a grass from the bank, Pansy chewed it to pulp, seeing or trying to see Nonna catching them red-handed with her blood up; she found it difficult to see it plainly.

'*They* don't know anything about Nonna,' Atalanta continued. 'When they asked if we were alone, I said we were. We *were* alone on the beach with Nonna in the harbour. I wanted to talk to Nonna before they did and by the time she got back they had gone, lock stock and barrel. I'm glad they don't know she exists; if some unknown quantity pounces suddenly from an unknown quarter it's obviously more efficacious than if it's half expected.'

Efficacious, Pansy wouldn't ask what it meant now. 'I see,' she said like Miss Lamb, but like Miss Lamb she didn't say what she saw.

'If the Rector's sensible, Nonna's going to make him go to the Workhouse with her and demand to see Leah. She means to get him to the cupboard if she can. If he's silly or out she's going to the Mayor or the Police. She can't bear cruelty. That's why she won't hang up fly-papers or set mousetraps or squash spiders. I'd have liked to have been in at the kill myself,' said Atalanta, 'but she made me go off to the train after you. You've been the most frightful nuisance.'

'I'm sorry,' said Pansy humbly; she knew a guest oughtn't to behave like that. 'I wish I'd never done it.'

'Don't be so lily-livered. Reforms are always a nuisance to somebody. Look at the Industrial Revolution – I bet that inconvenienced a lot of people.'

Pansy, who hadn't reached the Industrial Revolution in history yet, couldn't look at it very well but she didn't tell Atalanta so, and before she had said anything Atalanta went on to say something amazing: 'Let's hope you've started something that will reform all the Workhouses in the country.'

Pansy gasped with excitement, 'Do you think I have?'

Atalanta didn't answer that. She said crossly that she was hanged if she was going up the lane any further. 'You can see there's no stack over there –' she jerked her head towards the left where there was a flat cabbage field and beyond that a field of charlock. On the right was a cow field that sloped uphill. She was going across that, she said. There might be a stack over the other side or at any rate a view. She was fed up with walking.

Getting through the fence, the wire snagged a hole in Atalanta's frock. 'Who cares?' she said. She didn't. Pansy didn't think Nonna would, either. She didn't believe either of them would mend it. How lovely to be like that! At the thought of snagging Leah's frock, Pansy felt a sudden terrible responsibility fall on her like a bag of bricks. If you borrowed something you had to return it in good order. She had borrowed, not stolen, Leah's frock. If Matron found she had snagged it, anything might happen. Lying flat on her back, she edged herself under the wire.

The frock was safe for the moment, but following Atalanta, walking slowly because Leah's boot was hurting so badly, Pansy felt anxious for another reason: she was afraid Atalanta would give up before they found a stack and sleep where she fell. If she fell now she would fall into a cow pat. Pansy laughed rather loudly. She couldn't tell Atalanta how funny it was in case it made her think of stopping. Atalanta stumped on as though nothing had happened.

Pansy had just said 'There's a horse-fly on your back' when they reached the top of the field and saw what came next. There was a corn field; they were *making a stack*. They were loading the corn from the stooks on to a cart. Another full cart was by the stack and a man was pitchforking the corn on to the top of it. There were children playing about and two women sitting on the ground.

'They're making the stack for us!' cried Pansy excitedly. 'Shall we go and help?' She had forgotten everything for a moment: how she had ben trying to avoid strangers, how tired she was and how the boot hurt.

'Yes, if you want to let the cat out of the bag,' said Atalanta dampingly.

Pansy was unwilling to be damped; she felt devil-may-care. 'We needn't tell them anything; they'll be too busy to ask,' she argued, which wasn't very sensible as the women seemed to be doing nothing special, just sitting where it looked as though they might have had tea.

'Curiosity is one of the most powerful of all human emotions,' Atalanta said in her deep slow way.

Pansy knew, without asking, that she couldn't have made that up, how could she?

Atalanta sat down where she was, prepared to wait till the field was empty. Disappointed, but seeing the sense of what she said, Pansy sat down too. Staring at the field, she counted the stooks left. While they were collecting them she decided to take off Leah's boots for a bit, and the stockings too. How gorgeous to feel the cool grass on her feet! She felt as though her feet were two animals she had let out of prison.

When she looked up again she saw a dog running along sniffing the stubble. 'Look! – there's a dog sniffing,' she said in dismay. 'It can't be sniffing me, can it? We haven't been in the field, but do you think it will smell me out?'

'How can it from there? Don't be silly,' said Atalanta. 'And even if it came close and smelt you it wouldn't do anything about it. It's not a police dog, it's an ordinary farm collie.'

Pansy felt very relieved at hearing these comforting facts said aloud in Atalanta's deep positive voice.

The sun lay low over the field, making the shadows of the stooks very long. It had gone by the time the last sheaf had been tossed on to the stack. Then the harvesters went home. They unharnessed the dappled horse and left the cart behind. A boy and a little girl rode the horse led by a man. The cart with the white horse went away; children and a man sat on the back of it, their legs dangling. The other man perched on the side holding the reins. The women walked. The dog raced about till some one bellowed to it, then it too went. The field was empty.

'Now –' said Pansy, who had put on the boots again, ready. She left off the stockings; there was such a little way to go – at least it seemed very little after the long way she had come – that there wasn't time for the boots to rub too badly without them. She was so eager she could hardly wait for Atalanta. 'You walk slower than Aunt Susu,' she told her.

'When I'm her age I shan't walk at all; my thirty-six grandchildren will be pushing me in my Bath chair.'

'You'll get very fat – especially if you eat pork pies,' said Pansy. 'That's what the fat woman in the fair eats and she drinks stout. Grandfather says some of his patients –' but just then a hare streaked across the field putting an end to such fatty conversation.

'How do you think you're going to get on to the stack?' Atalanta inquired as though she had nothing to do with it.

Pansy said, 'Climb.'

'You can't climb up that.'

No, Pansy was afraid she couldn't. With a sinking heart she gazed at the stack which seemed to get higher with every step. If the cart had been close to it it might have helped although there would still have been a good climb left, but they had left it too far away. 'How did they get on to it?' Pansy wondered.

'They got on at the beginning and went up with it, of course. They could jump on to the cart when they wanted to get off while there was still some corn on it. One man did. But the other, who waited till all the corn was on the stack, didn't,' Atalanta said.

'What did he do?'

'Went down the other side. Didn't you see anything?'

'I can't look at everything at once and two of the boys were playing leap-frog,' Pansy said.

'Leap-frog! You'd be absolutely useless as a detective,' Atalanta told her.

'Grandfather says some of the very smallest things are important to detectives and spies.'

'Like disappearing down the other side,' said Atalanta mercilessly. 'Let's hope there's a ladder at the back.'

When they got to the stack and went round it, there *was* a ladder lying on the ground. There was a good view too.

They could see the way the harvesters had gone now; they were there, at the end of the long white track that ran down a gradual slope till it joined a road. The horse had turned in to the road already and was hidden by the hedge, the cart was just going. There were roofs and a church tower farther on. Below them, in a cup of the downs which fell away steeply here, was a big old house in a large garden. Beyond it, the downs were wooded.

'Elizabethan,' said Atalanta, looking at the house. 'It's built in the shape of an E.'

Pansy didn't mind what shape the house was; it was the stack she minded about. 'Come on, let's put the ladder up,' she urged. It was easier said than done, but they did it, and Pansy went up it first.

The top of the stack wasn't quite what she had hoped for. As she plodded along she had been picturing soft straw, or better still, lovely soft hay, but the heads of the corn made it lumpy and the stalks were stiff. It wasn't at all good for burrowing into, and now she came to think about it, she could not imagine why they made a stack of *corn*. She said as much to Atalanta when she arrived on top. 'The corn isn't threshed; they're wasting it all by making it into a stack.'

'Of course they won't waste it. They're stacking it to wait for the threshing machine,' Atalanta told her. 'It may not be threshed for ages – not till the winter.'

'I want to burrow,' Pansy said, 'and I don't see how we can in this.'

'I shall make a burrow.' Crouching down, Atalanta scooped up an armful of corn and laid it to one side. She pulled and scooped till she had made a hole big enough to lie in.

Pansy eyed the hole critically. 'The heads are still going to make it lumpy.'

'They would if I was going to lie on them.' Atalanta started methodically lining the burrow with stalks, spreading them across with the heads to the sides. When everything was ready, she stepped in, and beginning at her feet covered herself with corn till she was lying down blanketed to the chin.

'Is it comfy?' Pansy asked.

'Like a feather bed.'

Pansy, who had once slept on a feather bed, knew it wasn't like that at all, but it didn't matter. Eagerly, she started to make a burrow for herself.

11

TERROR IN THE NIGHT

WHEN Pansy woke up the moon was high in the sky. She had been so tired she had gone to sleep before it got up. Lying in the corn in the warm summer darkness, Atalanta had given her an examination on the constellations in the firmament of heaven. Pansy had found the Milky Way and Venus, but after that she hadn't found anything. And then she had remembered something that in all the stress of happenings she had forgotten to tell Atalanta. 'My fortune's come true! I've been among strangers and I've relied on my own resources and contrived to extricate myself with a certain amount of difficulty.'

'Nothing of the sort,' said Atalanta, 'George extricated you. If he hadn't let you out you'd have stayed with the meat till the butcher took you to the Workhouse and then you'd have been in the soup.'

'I extricated myself from Long Nose and Matron before that, when I ran away. I did it on my own, my own resources,' Pansy had pointed out.

Atalanta had said that by going to the butcher and getting shut up there she hadn't really extricated herself at all, she had simply leapt from the frying-pan into the fire. Pansy wouldn't agree that she hadn't extricated herself even if she hadn't been free for long. She couldn't bear to go among strangers and extricate herself again. Atalanta had argued that if she hadn't extricated herself already she couldn't extricate herself *again*. Atalanta could argue interminably when she felt like it, but luckily she had started having hiccups and got sick of it, 'If you want to interpret it that way –' she had said – 'it was only a *station fortune*.'

Yes, Pansy had wanted to interpret it that way. Lying under the moon, she still did most frightfully. It was all very well for Atalanta who only had her financial position to worry about. But suppose she was right? 'Suppose I do find myself among strangers again soon, will it be Long Nose and the police and dogs?' Pansy wondered. What she saw with her mind's eye made her miserably afraid, and then she managed to feel obstinate. Atalanta didn't know anything more about it than she did; it was *she* who had escaped and it was her fortune. Atalanta had been in an arguing mood. She said of course the pork pie hadn't given her hiccups when Pansy betted it had, and that Pansy didn't know what thirst was when of course she did, even if her tongue wasn't swollen and black.

She was still thirsty and very hot, covered in corn to her neck and with all her clothes on except for Leah's stockings and boots and the sun-bonnet. The boots and bonnet were near at hand, but the stockings she had hung out to air on a rung of the ladder. She was tickling horribly. Feeling her shoulder, she found it stringed with bites. Harvesters – she remembered what Aunt Katie had said to Ginie when her form was going to have tea in a hay field: 'I'll give you some carbolic soap and you had better rub yourself with that; you won't smell very nice but if you don't the harvesters will bite you to ribbons.' How awful! Thrusting aside the corn, Pansy sat up.

'Lie down,' said Atalanta.

'I can't,' said Pansy, surprised to find her awake, 'I'm being bitten to ribbons.'

'I *am* in ribbons. Lie down and be quiet, there's someone coming,' Atalanta hissed.

'Is it Long Nose?' Pansy whispered; her whole inside had churned up in fright.

'I don't know, but I've thrown the ladder down so that it won't look suggestive.'

Suggestive? 'I put the stockings –' Pansy began, but Atalanta told her to shut up. Very quietly because it was impossible not to, Pansy scratched first with one hand and then with the other. She squirmed inside and out, her head filled with unasked questions, her body covered with bites. Was it Long Nose? If it was and he put up the ladder again and came on to the stack what should they do? Should they push the ladder back before he got to the top of it? What about the stockings which weren't hers? Suppose it wasn't Long Nose and whoever it was went away, or it was Long Nose and he didn't find them, how were they going to get off the stack without the ladder?

There was the sound of feet, boots pricked by stubble. 'I'll wager she's round about in these fields somewhere,' said a man's voice.

'Let's 'ope 'unger brings 'er out into the open, sir,' said another.

Neither of them sounded like Long Nose, Pansy decided, but she could hardly have been more frightened if they had. Bites and all, her body stiffened like a post. They were after *her*, but hunger wouldn't bring her out. They didn't know she'd had some supper.

'H'm –' said the first voice, 'she's unlikely to be desperate yet.'

No, Pansy wasn't desperate for food and she wasn't so desperately thirsty that she would go out into the open for a drink, but the longing for a glass of water or some lemonade still stayed with her, in spite of her fear, like the tickling of her bites.

'They're beating the woods now, sir, but the lads from the camp will be along 'ere soon and they'll cover all the fields.'

'Good. She'll fight shy of the house, sure to – needn't worry about that.'

'Well, I'd best be getting back to the village, sir.'

Pansy heard the feet tramp off again. She got a little less like a post, but went on lying still except for furtive scratching. She heard a rustling as Atalanta moved.

'There they go,' Atalanta whispered. 'One's a policeman and the other's got a gun. He's not Long Nose.'

Pansy could hardly believe her ears; he had brought a gun to shoot *her* with. The terror of it swamped the relief that it really wasn't Long Nose. 'Don't let them see you,' she beseeched Atalanta hoarsely.

'They can't. Keep low and have a look, quick.'

Turning over, crawling low nearer the side of the stack, Pansy looked. They were going towards the gate through which the horse had gone. The man with the gun was shorter than Long Nose, shorter than the policeman. They went through the gate and disappeared.

'They couldn't shoot me; I didn't do much!' Pansy's lips trembled unexpectedly.

'I suspect there's more in it than one knows,' said Atalanta slowly. 'Something may have happened that they think is your fault.'

'What?' Pansy's voice sounded like a croak.

'I don't know, how can I?' said Atalanta reasonably. 'Or what's more likely I should think – Leah's run away and they're after her.'

'And the dogs have smelt her clothes which I've got on,' whispered Pansy miserably. 'But they hadn't got any dogs with them.'

'I dare say they've called them off now they've scented her so far; they may not want them to maul her and have tied them up somewhere.'

'Maul her – bite her and tear her to bits?' What Pansy saw she had seen before when she had thought of dogs on the cliff, but it made it no better.

'That's why they'd rather shoot, I expect.'

'They won't know the difference between me and Leah!' Pansy's voice trembled. She ought to mind as much about Leah as about herself, she knew, but in her fright she couldn't at the moment.

'That's your fault,' said Atalanta.

'You suggested changing clothes.'

'But you did it. They won't shoot to kill though, I shouldn't think,' Atalanta went on more kindly. 'They might try to wing you, I suppose, if you looked like getting away.'

'Wing?'

'Hit you without hurting you, in the leg or somewhere, to bring you down.'

'But it would hurt dreadfully,' said Pansy.

'I doubt if it would hurt more than being mauled, but it's no good fussing about it now,' said Atalanta. 'If you ask me there's something fishy somewhere. Even if Leah has run away – and Long Nose is bound to try and get her back because children aren't allowed to escape from Workhouses, and because she might expose him, too, which she jolly well would do if she'd got any sense – or if it's you he's after because he's a maniac and has set his heart on hunting you down, there wouldn't be such a *palaver*. That's what makes me think there's something worse, that someone's been murdered perhaps, and they think you did it.'

'No!' Pansy's voice was almost a screech, 'I didn't!'

'Don't make such a noise; you don't know who's lurking.'

'I didn't,' Pansy repeated in a hoarse whisper.

'I didn't suppose you did. I said they might think you had,' said Atalanta stolidly. 'You didn't push the butcher downstairs or anything, did you? Because if you did and he had a bad heart and was old he might have died of shock later on.'

No, Pansy hadn't. He'd gripped her, but she hadn't done anything to him except try to get away. She hadn't even kicked him, at least she didn't think she had; she hadn't on purpose anyway. 'I fought with George when he dragged me off. I kicked him and I pinched him too.'

That was unlikely to have killed *him* in Atalanta's opinion. Crossing her arms, she scratched both at once.

During this pause in the conversation Pansy tried to be braver, but when she thought of the dogs her courage ebbed again. 'Perhaps there aren't any dogs,' she suggested hopefully.

'You can't expect everything – dogs and Territorials.'

'*Territorials?*' In her surprise Pansy did not stop to point out that she didn't want the dogs.

'He said "The lads from the camp" – Territorials under canvas, sure to be,' said Atalanta knowledgeably. 'Leah must have murdered somebody, if its important enough to bring out the Territorials?'

'Oh – I don't think she would, not purposely,' said Pansy,

shocked. 'Do you think she's murdered Long Nose? Or Matron?'

Atalanta thought she would have had a good deal of difficulty, but on the other hand if she *had* been tortured. Or simply the thought of the cupboard might have goaded her to superhuman strength or cunning.

An owl hooting just then startled Pansy into speechlessness. Atalanta, who had been scratching her back, stopped. 'An owl,' she said then as if she had known it from the first minute. After a pause while Pansy recovered and did some scratching too, Atalanta said, 'I wonder if you had better give yourself up? If you haven't done anything worse than change clothes with Leah they'll find out their mistake.'

'No,' said Pansy appalled, 'I can't.' At the thought of it, of seeing Long Nose again, she seemed to shrink right down into the marrow of her bones. She didn't want to see the butcher, either. On the other hand she didn't want to be winged. 'If they saw me and were going to shoot it would be different. I could shout out that I'm not Leah and then if it's her they want everything would be all right and if it isn't and they want me then I'd have given myself up,' she explained. 'But I'd rather hide till they do see me. And then a happy thought struck her, 'By holding out I shall be helping Leah; it will give her more time to get away if it's her they want.'

Atalanta said that Leah never would escape. If they didn't find her in a day or two they would probably put her description in the paper.

'Or in the Post Office like they did when Canon Darling's dog was lost,' Pansy suggested.

'They may put yours – with your latest photograph if they can get it,' Atalanta said.

Pansy gasped and just then the owl hooted again; they knew what it was now, but it was very sudden all the same. The latest photograph was of Ginie and her and Boggles in their school clothes taken a year ago to send out to Mother and Father in India – the latest *proper* photograph that wasn't just a snap. She wasn't looking like that now, she thought, seeing with her mind's eye, seeing herself standing with her hands on Boggles's shoulders and Ginie with her hands on her shoulders. She looked very neat in her new purple coat and skirt and school boater with the purple riband with a madonna lily embroidered on it, but her face was the same she supposed, except that it was nearly a year older. She said as much to Atalanta and 'How would they get a photo?' she asked, when they didn't know where she lived. Atalanta saw no stumbling-block; they would track her to the Close. When Pansy said how worried the Aunts and Nana would be and perhaps Grandfather too a bit, Atalanta told her she should have thought of that before but she didn't suppose it would ever come to that at all.

'Why not?' Pansy asked, suddenly feeling rather flat.

'Because if you won't give yourself up – and it's you they're after – they'll find you before that I'll bet. If you don't want them to, we'd better go down to the house which they aren't going to bother about, before the Territorials arrive,' Atalanta advised. 'Once they swarm round here we're finished. Why the policeman didn't look on the stack I cannot imagine; I call it most frightfully careless.'

Pansy didn't care if he was careless, she was so glad he hadn't. Atalanta was peering over the side of the stack. 'It's a fair drop without a ladder.'

Pansy, who had crawled to peer too, agreed that it was.

'Which hand will you have?' Atalanta asked, 'If you choose the one with the bit of corn in it, you go. If it's empty you stay.'

'Left.'

Atalanta took her left hand from behind her back, opened it, then laid it on her lap. 'You go. Land on that heap of straw or corn or whatever it is there – turn round and drop with your face to the stack, and stretch out your arms as far as you can before you drop,' she said.

'You go, you know how,' Pansy urged.

'It's no good drawing lots if you don't abide by it.'

It wasn't, of course. Miserable as she was, Pansy knew that. 'Suppose I break my back and have to go about in a spinal carriage?' Pansy saw herself lying in a long basket-chair like the boy she had seen being pushed through the town, but she saw herself being pushed slowly through the Close by Nana or the Aunts; she didn't think they'd push her through the town.

'Don't be hysterical.'

It was as though Atalanta had thrown a jug of cold water over her and Pansy felt as angry as if she had. 'I'm not!' she hissed furiously.

'Then *go* before they come. If you can't drop a little way like that how are you ever going to climb the Alps? And if you marry a mountaineer he'll expect you to. Go *on*! Or would you prefer to wait for the Territorials?' Atalanta asked severely.

Pansy went suddenly, circumstances shaping her decision. It wasn't only because of the Territorials that she jumped when she did; she felt something crawling up her chest. The stack was *filled* with biting life. Pounding her chest with her fists to beat to death whatever was there, she jumped. She jumped plumb on to the pile face forwards and rolled over. Her back wasn't broken, she was all right. Atalanta's face was hanging above her, pale in the moonlight like an egg.

'You didn't jump the way I said. Put the ladder up,' Atalanta ordered.

How could Pansy by herself? 'I –' she began, and then she saw it – something dark moving along in the shadow of the hedge at the far side of the field. As she stared, motionless with terror, and Atalanta was saying 'Get a move on, do,' the thing came out of the shadow. Walking towards her in the moonlight was *a tall thin man in black*. As Pansy still stared, round-eyed with horror, as unmoving as if her feet had been nailed to the ground, something else came. Dashing up from behind the man, it came ahead of him, making a bee-line for the stack; it was a large black *dog*. There was another, too.

Pansy moved. In a hoarse, shrieking whisper, she hissed up the stack, '*Long Nose is coming with dogs!*' It was only a whisper but it seemed to ring across the field. Without waiting for Atalanta to answer, she fled.

She did not make for the open gate through which the policeman and the man had gone and the harvest people before them; it was too far to run in the open. She went straight through the fence by the stack on to the down, thrusting her way through the wire, tearing herself free with a rend of alpaca when it caught Leah's frock. A hare would have rushed down the steep slope without falling head over heels, but Pansy wasn't a hare and had to run in a scramble with her feet sideways and hurting as they were forced on edge inside the boots, but she was too frightened to care. If she could reach the house before she was caught she would be safe; she saw it as Tom Tiddler's ground. She thought she heard the dogs panting behind her but when she looked there was no sign of them and she realized the panting was her own. There was no sign of anyone. She could see the stack, a dark lump against the sky, but in the fleeting glance she gave it she couldn't see Atalanta; she must be lying low.

The down flattened out at the bottom before it reached the low stone garden-wall. It was so low Pansy got over it without difficulty. Crouching below it for a moment to get her breath, she looked again to see if Long Nose and the dogs were coming, but the down seemed empty still.

The garden sloped downhill again, but more gradually. It was the vegetable garden. Pansy recognized some carrots in the moonlight and, when she got up and ran down the path, she passed the dark spectral shapes of globe artichokes. Then it was flat again and there was a potting-shed casting a deep shadow over rows of onions. She was afraid of the shed, of what might lurk inside. Suppose she went in and Long Nose saw her, watching from up there on the down somewhere, as she scurried like a mouse in the moonlight? Skirting the potting-shed, slipping between two rows of sweet peas, she stopped again. Her breath was the only sound in the garden. Poking a little spy-hole in the sweet peas, she examined the down again. A little way from the stack, full in the moonlight, *was a tall black figure standing motionless by the fence gazing towards the garden*. Things moved on the down, weaving from side to side, racing to-

wards the bottom. *The dogs.* A whistle-shrilled. Jerking her face out from the sweet peas, Pansy turned and ran.

She ran out from between the two rows and tore down the path. Kicking over an empty watering-can, she pelted on to the great dark yew hedge at the end of the garden. There was no way through. Running across a bed, trampling spinach – the cool leaves brushing her legs – she reached the centre path. Here was the opening. Plunging through, she came out on to a pale narrow path leading away from the black shadow of the hedge across a great sea of grass. It led to a broad drive running straight up to the house, but Pansy did not want the drive. Racing across the grass, she got to the terrace without it. Panting up the steps, she flung herself on the iron ring handle of the great wooden door. It might be locked because it was the night, or the owner might be up still because of the chase. If only she could get in and hide. If the dogs came now she'd be caught against it and torn to pieces. The big iron ring was not easy to turn. Her breath came in little sobs as she struggled frantically. Just as she had turned it right round and was going to push, a voice behind her called, 'Good evening. Can I help?'

Pansy jumped in her skin. Looking round, she saw a man coming towards her across the terrace. He wasn't Long Nose; he was quite little. 'Yes, please, please, I want to get in, the dogs are coming, they've smelt me out, he's after me with them!' Her voice rose.

'Then I think you should come in, most certainly.' Taking the handle from her, he opened the door quite easily and let her in.

12

FACES AT THE WINDOW

It was a big hall, lit only by the dim light of a lamp on the table in the middle and by some moonlight which came through a window half-way up the great dark staircase. As the man closed the door and bolted it, Pansy felt an enormous relief. He had locked out the dogs and Long Nose, if only he didn't let them in. *Let them in* her mind repeated, making her horribly afraid again. Who was this man? Was he a friend or an enemy? Almost at once, as she thought about his smallness, she knew: he was the man they had seen with the policeman, he was after her, *he was an enemy*. He would give her to Long Nose and the dogs. Her breath sucked up on its own. 'I'm not who you think I am,' she said. Then she knew it mightn't be true. He might not think she was from the Workhouse in spite of her clothes. He might know it was her they were looking for in Leah's clothes.

'How do you know what I think?' Going over to the lamp, he turned it up. It was a tall lamp and gave quite a lot of light like that, but the hall was so big, the edges and the stairs where the moon wasn't were still dark. 'Let's have a look at you.'

While he was looking at her, Pansy looked at him. He had quite an ordinary kind of face; he wasn't *like* anything. Her friend, the Judge, was like a tortoise, but this man wasn't bald like the Judge, and he hadn't got a lot of white hair like the Bishop; he had some quite ordinary hair. She quite liked his face, but that didn't mean he wasn't an enemy. Some of the Boers in the Boer War were certain to have had nice faces, Aunt Katie had said. He was small and thin and old, though not as old perhaps as Grandfather. He had on a brown suit. 'How do you know what I think?' he repeated.

'I don't,' said Pansy unhappily. 'I did think you'd think I was Leah, but I see now you mightn't.'

'I don't know anyone called Leah. I've only known one Leah in my life and that was a cook we had when I was seven. She used to eat raw meat.'

'*Raw?*'

'Swallowed it down in lumps like a dog.'

The word *dog* pulled up Pansy, putting a stop to the extraordinary picture she was seeing with her mind's eye. 'Please don't let the dogs in,' she implored.

'What dogs? You aren't being hunted by a pack of hounds are you?'

'I don't know. I haven't seen a pack, but there are two on my heels.'

'Then they should be here by now.' The man cocked his head. 'I can't hear yelping, can you?'

No, Pansy couldn't, she told him truthfully, but this fact didn't make her feel much safer.

'Who's chasing you?' he asked, as if he hadn't already discussed things with the policeman.

Pansy came out with it, 'Long N–, the Master of the Workhouse, I've just seen him watching me.'

'Ah – so it's there you come from.'

'No, I don't, but these clothes belong to someone who does, I think he thinks I've stolen them but I haven't, I've only borrowed them,' said Pansy rather loudly, 'and I'm going to send them back.' She remembered then about tearing the dress on the fence – which she hadn't had time to investigate – but decided not to mention it. She did not mention having had any stockings or a bonnet, either. She had remembered about them when she was in the garden; the stockings must have fallen off the rung of the ladder when Atalanta pushed it down and the bonnet was on the stack. She hadn't had time to worry about them then, but now she felt appalled. She hoped Atalanta would find them.

He examined her again, briefly. 'I shouldn't bother; they aren't worth sixpence. You haven't even got any stockings.'

'I had,' said Pansy wretched, 'I left them by the stack, and the sun-bonnet. He won't believe me if he gets me now. He'll kill me!' She was being like Leah and she couldn't help it.

'Hardly, I should think, for a pair of stockings and a bonnet and that frock and boots. He's not hunting you down for those things, you can take my word for it. Either he's mad or you've been up to something worse.'

'I haven't done much. Atalanta thinks he thinks I've done something which I haven't – murdered someone, but I haven't, not purposely. I never did anything to the butcher and if he's died of shock since it wasn't because of anything I did to him, it would only have been the surprise of finding me when he put down his hand for the tin of beastliness – or crossness because I'd escaped.'

'Bitcher, murder, Atalanta – you'd be no earthly good as a dog; you'd never keep your nose to the scent. Are you hungry?'

Yes, Pansy was. 'I had tea, well really I suppose it was supper, with a herbalist, but I've done a great deal since then.'

'I've done a good deal since dinner too,' the man said. 'We'll go and have a look in the larder. The maids are in bed and my wife is away. I can't promise you any herbs I'm afraid, but there should be some cold sirloin left, and if your butcher's dead there's no knowing when you'll have another joint.'

'He wasn't our butcher,' Pansy explained.

It was quite a long way to the larder. The man went ahead with a small lamp which he had lit on purpose. There was enough light to see by, but not anything like enough to fill up corners. As Pansy followed him along a broad passage and then through a door and down some dark stairs, she remembered that he was supposed to be an enemy. Perhaps he was taking her to the cellar to imprison her there. Terrified, she stopped walking at the bottom of the stairs.

He stopped too. 'Come on,' he said.

'Where are we going?' Pansy's voice died into a whisper.

'I told you – the larder.'

'How do I know that – that you aren't an enemy?'

'If I was I shouldn't be taking you to the larder. If you don't come, you'll be swallowed up in darkness. You'll go round and round like a bat.'

'Atalanta says bats can find their way.'

'So they can, but if you don't want to come to the larder where will you find your way to? It's no good going outside to be torn to bits by dogs, not to mention the man who's after your clothes,' he pointed out. 'What's more, this is my house and if I invite you to the larder you should have the good manners not only to accept, but to come.'

How dreadfully rude she had been! Pansy's face got scarlet in the gloom. "I'm sorry,' she said humbly. 'I didn't mean to be rude. I want to come to the *larder* very much, I only thought –' how could she say what she had thought?

'I know exactly what you thought,' he said as they started off again, 'you thought that I was taking you down to the cellar to lock you up.'

'Are you a fortune-teller?' Pansy asked with wonder.

'No; it was quite a commonplace conjecture, but untrue as it happens. It would be pointless for me to lock you in the cellar when I don't want your frock or your boots and you wouldn't be at all happy down there with the black-beetles.'

'No, I shouldn't!' said Pansy quickly and very loudly.

There was the cold sirloin in the larder, and the remains of a plum tart and a rice pudding, and some cold baked potatoes, a bowl of dripping, and a large Stilton cheese like Grandfather's. Pansy chose dripping, and her host sirloin and pickled onions. Pansy asked if she could have some water. He offered her milk, but she stuck to water. She was so thirsty she would have liked to bury her face in a water trough and take great mouthfuls like a horse. He would get some from the scullery, he said. When they had found the bread for Pansy's dripping in a bin under the larder shelf, they went to the kitchen where he lit the gas. The scullery led out of the kitchen which was convenient for the water, and while he filled a jug from the dresser, Pansy laid the plates. When they had got some knives and a fork for him and one for the onions, they sat down at the big wooden table to eat and drink.

The dripping was delicious. 'Atalanta loves dripping – pork specially.' As this was beef Pansy rather wished she hadn't mentioned pork, particularly as she liked pork best too. 'I love beef,' she added hastily which was quite true. 'I wonder what Atalanta's doing.'

'Who is Atalanta? Why do the people you know have such outlandish names? It must be a confounded nuisance,' he said, 'to have a name like that.'

'Confounded,' Pansy agreed. 'Atalanta hates it, but her father reads Greek mythology and she's called after Atalanta.'

'Arcadian huntress – does she go in for boar hunting like her namesake?' he asked. 'Is she a sprinter?'

Pansy knew what he meant, he meant an animal boar not a Boer like the Boers in the Boer War. 'No, I shouldn't think she's hunted a boar; she's never said so,' she told him, 'and she isn't a sprinter, she won't run.'

His name was Wellington. He had been called after the Duke of Wellington; his father had served under him at the Battle of Waterloo. His grandfather had been a soldier too, and so was he.

'Fancy your father being at Waterloo,' said Pansy, impressed.

'My groom fought in the Crimea. He lost a hand from frost-bite there,' he told her. When Pansy asked if he had been in the charge of the Light Brigade which she had just learnt a poem about, he said no, he hadn't. He would probably have been killed if he had been.

Pansy agreed. 'Have you ever had to ride *Into the jaws of Death, into the mouth of Hell*?' she asked.

'Not absolutely into the *jaws*,' he said.

> *'Cannon to right of them,*
> *Cannon to left of them,*
> *Cannon in front of them,*
> *Volley'd and thunder'd;*

Stormed at with shot and shell,
Boldly they rode and well,
Into the jaws of Death,
Into the mouth of Hell
 Rode the six hundred.'

Pansy had started reciting, and he had joined in at the second *cannon* and they had gone on together from there. When it was over – and as she had forgotten the beginning of the next verse, she didn't try to go further for the present – she said, 'I didn't know you knew it.'

'You didn't ask me.'

'It must have been awful. I do hope you won't have to do that.' The dreadful vision of her companion being *stormed at with shot and shell* was made worse by the way he was enjoying his sirloin and onions.

'Unlikely now,' he reassured her. 'I'm a general for one thing, and generals usually do the arranging, not the charging, and I wouldn't arrange for my soldiers to do what the Light Brigade had to if I could help it.'

'*Someone had blunder'd.*'

'They shouldn't have.'

That's what Pansy thought, but she had stopped caring about it for the moment. 'Are you really a *general?*'

Skewering a little onion with his fork, he began gently to pull it out of the bottle. 'You sound incredulous; isn't it all right?'

Pansy, who had been gazing at him, flushed. Looking away, she reached for the salt and sprinkled her dripping again, which she had done once already. Then she scratched a bite under the table just above Leah's left boot which really did need scratching.

'Do you think I'm too small?' he asked pleasantly. Putting the onion on a thin strip of pink meat which was pink because it hadn't been cooked enough, he rolled it up deftly like a baby in a shawl and spearing the bundle with his fork he put it in his mouth. 'Size is not absolutely necessary – look at dogs; a terrier will catch nine times the number of rats a St Bernard will.'

'Yes –' Pansy agreed eagerly, 'it's the same with vege-
tables; they always send giant carrots and peas and things
to shows but most of them are much too big and coarse to
eat, Aunt Katie says.'

'Good; well that point's proved. Now tell me – who are
you and what have you been up to?'

Pansy started to tell him everything. She had got as far as
the bit about the beastly boy grabbing her food when the
bell rang. She almost jujmped out of her skin. 'What's that?'

'A bell,' the General said, 'one of those up there –' he
jerked his head at a row of bells hanging above the door.
'Looks to me like the second from the left; it's waggling,
but we'll soon see.' Getting up, he went over to look at the
indicator on the wall which showed which bell had rung.
'Odd time to call at after one o'clock in the morning.'

Pansy, who had found her voice, said, 'It's Long Nose!
Don't let him in, please don't!'

'Front door, I thought so,' said the General.

'Can't we pretend that everyone's in bed?'

'No, whoever it is has seen the light in the hall I expect.
It may not be Long Nose; it's probably that friend of yours,
Atalanta. You don't want to keep her on the step all night,
do you?'

No, Pansy didn't, but she didn't think Atalanta would
ring the bell.

'I think, from what I've heard of her,' the General said,
'she would.'

'It's Long Nose with the dogs!' Pansy persisted frantically. 'He was on the down watching me when I was in the
garden; the police are after me too and the Territorials. We
heard the policemen tell you – it was you, wasn't it? – the
lads were coming to cover the fields.'

The General laughed suddenly. 'You poor little idiot – it's
not you they were after! They were looking for a lioness
which had escaped from a circus van. They've got her now,
caught her in the woods, and the Territorials have been
called off.'

'Do you mean everyone wasn't hunting for me? Or
Leah?' Pansy asked unbelievingly.

'I'm afraid not.' He sounded apologetic. 'But I expect you're glad. You weren't enjoying being hunted much, were you? You'd had about enough.'

'Yes,' Pansy agreed, meaning she had had enough. She did feel relieved, but she felt a little flat too – like a bottle of fizzy lemonade that has just had the cork taken out. Then she remembered that she *was* being chased by Long Nose who was standing outside the front door now, and she was afraid again. When she told the General that he was chasing her still, that it had nothing to do with the lion, he asked if she were sure. 'Did you really see him?'

'Yes,' she said.

Just then there was a tapping noise; it came from behind the red curtains.

'Someone's tapping on the window. Go and peep between the curtains and see if it's him,' the General ordered. 'I don't know the fellow by sight so it's no good me going.'

'I can't,' whispered Pansy, petrified with terror.

'Of course you can. Hunger makes cowards of us all, but after all that bread and dripping you've no excuse,' the General told her brutally. 'I'll turn down the gas and then he can't possibly see you. Go on.'

As Pansy went slowly towards the window the light went down. It was dreadful. She couldn't do it. She stopped.

'Go on,' said the General.

Clenching her hands and biting hard on her lower lip, she crept forward again. Close to the curtains, her courage was just giving out again when she remembered the charge of the Light Brigade; this helped to stiffen her. Pulling aside the curtains very gently, she made a tiny crack just big enough to peer through.

It was dark in the shadow of the house and there were bushes. Close to the window stood two people; one was Atalanta, and the other, his hand gripping Atalanta's shoulder, was a tall black – letting go the curtain, drawing back as though a wasp had stung her, Pansy turned and fled across the kitchen to where the General stood waiting under the gas. 'It's him with Atalanta! He's got her by the shoulder!' she whispered hoarsely.

'He has, has he?' said the General calmly. 'We'd better man the guns. No –' he turned up the gas, 'I think we won't fire immediately, we'll carry out a strategic *coup*. You go and hide in the larder.'

'I'm not afraid,' said Pansy. She had begun to tremble rather badly, but she tried not to let it show.

'Then that makes everything easier, but I still think we should have a *coup*,' the General said.

There was more tapping on the window, louder now.

'Go on, I'm just going to open up.' The General moved towards the window.

'Atalanta –' Pansy began.

'Leave her to me; I'll save Atalanta. She's too accomplished a strategist to be allowed to perish, though I dare say she's quite capable of extricating herself. Go.'

Pansy went. She went into the larder and shut the door. She hadn't got any light and as she was hiding she mustn't have one naturally, but it was a relief to see a faint glimmer of moonlight filtering through the little round holes in the wire window. She didn't like being alone in there, it made her think of Leah's cupboard; it was bigger than a cupboard, but smaller than the butcher's room. If Long Nose beat the General, he might come and lock her in. With Atalanta on the General's side it would be two to one, but would Atalanta know the General was a friend? – would she know before it was too late? If she did, would she have a chance to help him? 'I'd better lock *myself* in if I can,' thought Pansy, 'till I know what's happening.'

There was no key inside, and when she opened the door very quietly she found there wasn't one outside, either. Long Nose couldn't lock her in, but she couldn't lock him out. This made her feel very insecure. Shutting the door again, she looked for somewhere to hide; the only place was behind the bread-bin under the shelf in the corner. But instead of feeling safer when she was settled there, she felt like a cornered rat. She wasn't really hidden either, the bin wasn't big enough. If he brought a candle, he'd find her. She couldn't stay there cornered.

She was just going to crawl out again when she heard

124

footsteps approaching. They were coming from the kitchen way. Long Nose? No, it was the General, Pansy thought; he had come out of the kitchen and was going somewhere – where? Was he going to let Long Nose and Atalanta in at the back door?

She made no sound as the steps went past the larder. She heard them go on down the passage, making her feel abandoned and isolated in this big unknown house, seeing the dark passage and dark stairs down which they had come, the door leading to that other passage, and the great hall and staircase going up past the moonlight into darkness. Holding her breath, she strained her ears to listen. There was such quietness around her she seemed to hear her own listening. She swallowed and the swallow seemed to fill the larder. She couldn't hear the footsteps any longer. Then she heard the opening of a distant door, and the murmur of voices. They had come.

There were steps again, more steps. As they came nearer, Pansy thought of the General talking to the policeman in the field. Suppose, in spite of the dripping and everything, he *was* the enemy after all? Suppose he had been leading her on like the worst kind of spy, playing with her like a cat with a mouse, a *double game*, and now he and Long Nose had Atalanta in their power and were coming to corner her in the larder where he'd sent her on purpose to wait to be caught? What an idiot she'd been! She felt hot with fury and fright. She wouldn't wait to be caught. She'd go and hide somewhere else and come back and save Atalanta later.

It was too late. The steps were nearly at the door. They reached it. They stopped.

'She's in there,' said the General's voice.

The door was flung open.

Crushed into the corner, Pansy bowed her head, pushing her chin down on to her chest between her hunched shoulders.

'Where?' said a man's voice.

Pansy's heart seemed suddenly to lurch into stillness.

Feet came nearer. 'Behind the bin,' said Atalanta.

How *could* she! Pansy couldn't believe it. Lifting her head, she saw Atalanta's dark lumpish shape in the dimness, and behind her, filling up the doorway, his head bent to get under it because he was so tall, the thin black –

'Beast! –' said Pansy almost choking, 'you confounded beast!'

'Don't be silly,' said Atalanta. 'Here's these. You can carry them now, I'm sick of them!' She plumped down Leah's stockings and sun-bonnet next to the cheese.

13

VISITORS IN THE SPARE ROOM

They had another feast, all sitting round the kitchen table –
Pansy, Atalanta, the General and the Vicar, or rather Pansy
and the General continued the feast they had left off, and
Atalanta and the Vicar started in fresh. The Vicar had sirloin and no onions, and Atalanta had dripping and onions.
Pansy wished she'd had onions with her dripping, but after
the business of looking silly in the larder she still felt a bit
on her high horse with Atalanta and too proud to be a copy-
cat.

Seeing the Vicar there, eating his meat, with the gas
turned up, his kind face beaming, it was difficult to think
how he could ever have looked like Long Nose although
really Pansy quite understood how it had been. He was tall
and thin and dressed in black like Long Nose, and she
hadn't seen his face in the hay field and she hadn't seen it
through the kitchen window, not properly, because of the
dark. and because she had been too frightened to look she
was so sure it was Long Nose. She had leapt to conclusions –
that's what Aunt Katie would say. He *had* got a long
nose, but it wasn't like Long Nose's; it was fatter, more like
a donkey's, she thought now examining him closely, but he
looked cleverer than a donkey.

While they feasted everyone explained things. Atalanta
explained how she had seen the Vicar from the stack, seen
that he wasn't Long Nose, that he was a clergyman. He had
come close to the stack and stood in the moonlight and she
had seen his dog-collar for one thing. She had asked him to
put up the ladder for her to get down.

'Why couldn't you jump like I did?' said Pansy.

'Why should I when there was help at hand?' said Atalanta reasonably. While he was putting up the ladder a boy had shouted across the field, 'They've got 'er, sir!' When the Vicar had called, 'Where?' the boy had shouted back, 'In the woods!' The Vicar had said, 'So that's that; we can all go home now,' and had finished hoisting up the ladder. Atalanta knew, she said, that Pansy couldn't have reached the woods so soon. 'I knew what I'd already suspected; that they were chasing you or Leah.'

'No, you didn't!' said Pansy bluntly, and then because you couldn't flatly contradict in front of a General and a Vicar, she had added, 'I don't believe.'

'Don't be idiotic,' said Atalanta who seemed to have no scruples about the General and the Vicar, 'how can you know how my mind was working when you weren't there? You aren't psychic.'

Pansy was opening her mouth to say 'how do you know?' when the Vicar said that he was thankful that she wasn't. It made her feel better at once, as though by her own efforts she had escaped being what Aunt Katie called 'extremely undesirable'.

When the Vicar had told Atalanta about the lioness, she said it was pointless to be secretive any longer.

Secretive – in spite of being cross with her, Pansy, who had just put a large piece of bread and dripping in her mouth, stopped biting and gazed at Atalanta with unwilling admiration. How did she know all the words she knew?

'At least it was unnecessary to pretend you didn't exist, and we came down to the house together to look for you. I said you'd got tired of the stack, I didn't go into all the rigmarole about the Workhouse – although I knew I'd have to if we found you,' said Atalanta; 'you look so awful.'

'I know.' Pansy pressed her bare knees together under the table and started up another itch by mistake.

'It's always better not to be dressed too gaudily when you're on the run,' said the General. 'Now begin at the beginning again and tell us the whole story. The Vicar hasn't heard the earlier part.'

Pansy, who had just found some scrumptious brown gravyish dripping left under the fatty pale bit on her plate and was planning to eat it by itself and not mash it up with the rest and get an onion if she could reach for the bottle when Atalanta wasn't looking, abandoned her activities rather wistfully till later.

She began at the bit when she saw the Workhouse party on the beach.

'You haven't begun at the very beginning, you haven't explained that we'd come to Crackingbourne for the day; it makes quite a difference later on,' Atalanta said. 'If we'd been staying in Crackingbourne we wouldn't have had to work our way along the coast.'

Had they really been doing that? It sounded so much better than walking along the cliff, Pansy thought. But Atalanta was right. She started again at the point where they had left Longspit in the gig with Mr Chubb and she had on her own blue and white striped cotton frock. It seemed almost impossible now that this morning could have belonged to today, that it had been going on before they ever got into the gig. This very morning she had gone to the churchyard with Nonna and done her good deed carrying the camp-stool there and back without dreaming of the deed that was to come, and before that there had been breakfast and getting up.

There was a good deal of interruption as Pansy went along. Atalanta made corrections and added things she left out; the General cut in to get things straight and comment on strategy; and when it came to what went on in the Workhouse, the Vicar murmured, rather as if he were talking to himself, 'Pussy will soon get to the root of things, he'll dig out the truth.' How could a cat dig out the truth? Pansy stared at him in wonder for a moment; Atalanta blinked at him; the General shot him a glance, but no one asked him what he meant and Pansy went on.

According to the General, it had been bad strategy to hide under the butcher's counter. "You were cornered, unarmed, bound to be ambushed sooner or later.'

'But where else could I go?' asked Pansy.

'Down a side-street, double back and outflank the enemy.'

'I don't think there was a side-street before the shop,' said Pansy slowly, trying to remember.

'Then you should have flattened yourself in a doorway. You could rely on the charging enemy to look ahead.'

The Vicar knew all about Willie Stacey, the herbalist. They had grown up in the same village, Puddle Monkton, fifteen miles away, where the Vicar's father had been Rector for thirty years. Stacey's father had been of good blood, an eccentric and a poet of sorts. His mother had come of gipsy stock and according to the villagers rode over the sea on a broomstick on moonlight nights. When Willie was six she had ridden away for good.

'Did you see her go?' asked Pansy breathlessly.

No, the Vicar hadn't; he had only been five when she went for good.

'Did she really ride on a broomstick?'

'How could a broomstick fly?' said Atalanta. 'Surely you've done gravity, Pansy?'

Yes, of course, Pansy had. She had known about it before she ever got to school – that if it wasn't for gravity pressing down on the earth's surface everyone would float straight up into the sky and the gravity that kept them in place pushed down broomsticks too. But

'But it is an exciting vision, the figure on a broomstick flying black in a moonlit sky over a silver sea, and, without visions, life,' said the Vicar, 'would be a drab affair indeed.' He went on to say that Willie lived alone in the same tumbledown house in Puddle Monkton still with sixteen cats.

How could he be alone with sixteen cats? Was it one of those that was going to dig out the truth? Leaving the matter unsolved, Pansy finished telling about the herbalist, went on to the couple and the tandem, till she reached Atalanta. From there, she and Atalanta went on, first one and then the other, and sometimes rather loudly together. It was when she came to jumping off the stack, when Atalanta had said, 'Which hand will you have?' that a sudden thought struck Pansy.

'You never showed me the corn in your hand. You just opened it quickly and put it in your lap.

'There wasn't any,' said Atalanta coolly.

'But it's the hand with something in it that counts. I chose the left. If you had the corn in your right hand it was for you to jump.'

'Both were empty.'

Pansy was too angry to bother about the General and the Vicar. 'Cheat!' she said furiously.

'There was no cheating about it; you didn't ask.'

'You know what I *mean*.'

'Yes, perfectly,' said the Vicar.

'Tactics,' murmured the General.

When all was told, even to the history of the lioness's escape which the Vicar had had straight from the fairground man himself, the General reviewed the situation. 'Long Nose isn't chasing you, Pansy; you can take my word for it. He's got something better to do – or should have,' he said bluntly.

'Do you mean I've been running away for nothing?' Pansy gazed at him rather forlornly.

'I've just told you,' said Atalanta.

'Well, I haven't! I may have been lately, but he did send boys to catch me at the beginning and if I hadn't run away I'd have been caught. *You* would have been; you wouldn't have run fast enough.'

Putting some bread and dripping in her mouth, Atalanta blinked sleepily. 'I shouldn't have started; I should have handled things differently.'

'He sent boys to catch you at the beginning, yes,' said the General, sticking to his point, 'but after you got away – and I expect he gave the boys a dressing-down for letting you give them the slip – he'd have called off the hunt, I'm certain.'

'But suppose someone's died and they think I've killed them?'

'Why should anyone have died?' The General had finished his sirloin and, pushing his plate away, he put his elbows on the kitchen table and clasped his hands.

'It's what I suggested when it looked as though everyone was after Pansy,' Atalanta said, 'but now of course it doesn't hold water.'

'None,' agreed the General.

'And if they were chasing the lioness it doesn't mean Leah's run away or murdered anyone, either,' Pansy said slowly.

Atalanta lazily cut an onion in half and said, 'Of course not.'

'So no one's running away now,' said Pansy, feeling a little flat in the bottom of her heart again.

'The fact remains you did get away through your own initiative – not a bad effort on the whole,' the General told her, 'and I'll wager Long Nose would like to wring your neck if he got the chance, which he won't.'

Pansy, who had swelled up at this praise, felt her spirits sinking again at the awful thought.

'I expect he's lost interest now,' the Vicar said. 'But I haven't lost interest in him. I've got nothing to do with the Workhouse, it's not in my parish, but I intend to find out if that child's telling the truth.'

'I am,' Pansy said, hurt.

'Not you –' he smiled at her – 'the child Leah. If those children are really frequently beaten and shut up in a cupboard for minor offences then the sooner there is a thorough investigation the better. But Pussy will be on to it by now if he's seen your grandmother. He was only inducted a week ago, but I've yet to see the grass grow under Pussy's feet.'

Pansy was still at sea over Pussy, she did not know what *inducted* meant, and Nonna was Atalanta's grandmother not her own, who had died long before she was born when her own mother was a child. Atalanta said nothing, continuing to eat slowly and composedly, and it was left to Pansy to put the business straight. She was just opening her mouth to do so when the General spoke. 'The Vicar's alluding to Mr Pussyfoot, the new Rector of Holy Trinity, Crackingbourne.'

The Vicar nodded. 'Always call him "Pussy"; we were at

school together. He'll make no bones about having the Master on the mat – the whole Governing Body if necessary; he specializes in the persecuted.'

'Good. I don't envy the Master his job, mind you; running a pauper show can't be all beer and skittles and some of those children, poor little blighters, can be devils I'll bet, but if that fellow's a bully I'd like to see him do pack-drill.'

Pack drill. Pansy's eyes, that had been gazing at the General, flopped shut. She had had a very tiring day and the dripping seemed to be having a sleepy effect on her. She opened them and sat up straighter, but the lids fell down again almost at once. She woke up to hear the General saying, 'You can sleep in the double spare room.'

'We're sleeping on a stack,' Pansy's voice sounded blurred.

'You can't go back there tonight. Besides, you'll be bitten to rags again,' he told her.

'Ribbons,' said Atalanta in her deep voice. It sounded more collected than she looked; she looked as untidy as Pansy, but in a more distinguished way, due to her pomegranate frock which she had put on again today after spilling a plate of stewed rhubarb in the lap of her pink check yesterday. The pomegranates were dirty, the whole frock was, and very crumpled, but it still contrived to have a more distinguished air than the torn, dishevelled, hideously ugly and thoroughly filthy grey alpaca. Atalanta's sand-shoes were even dirtier than her dress; wetted by the sea, they had picked up a quantity of dust, and although she hadn't fallen into a cow-pat her right foot had trodden in one; not that her feet were visible, they were under the table. Her snood had slipped nearly off the back of her head, whiskers hung round her ears, her fringe was hooked behind her spectacles again, and her pigtails looked like a twist of garden bast from which gardeners had violently dragged strands in all directions. She was tired too, but her eyes were not absolutely closed; the lids dropped half-way down like window-blinds that have got hitched up or been only partially pulled down to keep out the sun. This made her look broody, like a hen.

'Ribbons then,' the General said. As Pansy and Atalanta followed him upstairs a few minutes later, after saying good night to the Vicar, he said that as so much of the night was gone it was not worth while to wake one of the maids. Ten to one the bed was made up; if it wasn't they could sleep in the blankets.

The bed *was* made up, but there was no water in the washstand jug. 'Cut out washing and rinse down when you get up,' he ordered.

Pansy was awake enough to think that would suit Atalanta down to the ground. She went on saying 'down to the ground' to herself while she held the lamp for Atalanta to see to light the candle.

'Sleep tight,' the General said as he left them.

'I shall sleep tight in my vest,' Pansy said when he had gone.

Atalanta didn't say anything. Taking off her spectacles, she yawned with a cracking sound.

Pansy sat down on the edge of a chair and let her feet out of prison again. She let out some corn as well. She could not see much detail even with the candle and moon. It was a big room and the candlelight was not nearly enough, but she knew what she had already seen in the cow-field, that her feet were not clean; it was the fault of those stockings. 'Do you think we shall make the sheets dirty?'

'Who cares?' Atalanta was clawing her frock over her head and her voice was muffled.

Pansy remembered what Florrie had said to Rose in the spare room when Grandfather's professor friend had stayed a night at the Close. 'The bed looked as though a wild animal had slept in it, sheets all topsy-turvy, looked as if they'd been put through a mangle, you wouldn't credit.' If they lay stiff, they wouldn't be like dirty wild animals, only dirty, thought Pansy, wrenching off Leah's frock. She had never been so glad to be out of anything, even the boots. Now she was herself with nothing but her own clothes on. 'I don't know how I can bear to put the frock on again in the morning,' she said.

'You'll reap what you've sown.' Atalanta, who hadn't even taken off her petticoat, got on to the bed.

'Aren't you going to undress any more?' Pansy asked.

No, Atalanta wasn't. Pushing back the blankets, Atalanta lay down on her back under the sheet and shut her eyes so that the lids came right down. The sheet made her look dead, deader than when she was being the Lady of Shalott. 'We can't brush our teeth or wash out our mouths with water as we haven't got any toothbrushes or water,' Pansy said. She knew Atalanta didn't mind, but she did wish she would say something so that although she looked dead it would be plain she wasn't. But Atalanta neither spoke nor moved. Pansy left her hair as it was; the General had picked out the straw. No one had drawn the curtains so there was nothing to draw back. Opening the window, she looked out. She could see the downs and the top of the stack in the moonlight. She had wanted to sleep in a stack all night so much; she wished she had, even if it hadn't been very comfortable. Scratching her waist, she blew out the candle and got into her side of the bed. The springs didn't screech like the springs in Mrs Chubb's bed. It was much bigger. There was no need to touch each other at all if they kept to their own sides, but she did poke Atalanta very lightly to find out if she was dead. She was warm and made a little gobbling noise. Relieved, Pansy lay down flat on her back and went almost straight to sleep.

14

COFFEE, APRICOTS AND A HOOK

She woke up again before it was light. Atalanta was sitting up scratching her neck. Pansy started in on her ribs at once. 'Do you think we've still got them?' she asked.

'Of course. Can't you feel any fresh bites?'

Yes, Pansy could; she had been scratching her waist, not her ribs, when she got into bed. 'If only we'd had a bath, they'd have drowned.'

'No, they wouldn't, they'd have gone up into our hair if they'd had any sense.'

'We ought to get right under water – dive into the sea; you could dive and I could just get under without my cap.' Seeing with her mind's eye all the harvesters swimming off the top of her head, imagining the clean cool loveliness of the sea, filled Pansy with longing. Not that she was hot; she wasn't. She was cold, tickling, and dirty.

'I've taken off everything and shaken my vest,' Atalanta said.

'Have you?' Pansy looked at her in amazement.

'There are no matches and I couldn't see if anything fell out.'

Pansy told her there was a box in the candlestick and Atalanta said she knew and it was empty; she'd used the last one to light the candle before. Pansy saw that the moon had gone. Getting out of bed, she shook her own vest. She didn't see anything fall out, either. They went to sleep again under both the blankets.

They were still asleep when Nellie, the parlourmaid, came in at half past eight with two cans of water. This gave her a chance to stare her fill, without being rude, at whoever was in the bed. The General's orders had been explicit but brief. 'Two ladies in the double spare room; they will breakfast with me at nine o'clock and they won't require any early morning tea;' that was all he'd said. You could have knocked her down with a feather. Two middle-aged maiden ladies was what she'd expected, though where they'd come from unbeknownst at that time of night, and unbeknownst they must have come seeing that he'd never so much as mentioned them before, she couldn't imagine. That accounted for the clutter on the kitchen table that had made Maud so cross, though why there had been four places, and why two ladies should want to eat meat and dripping and onions – dripping if you please – in the middle of the night was beyond her. And now there were these two!

The bed looked as though they'd been fighting hammer and tongs all night. Bitten too. Something had walked all across the bigger one's neck, biting as it went. Sleeping in her vest she was. As for the other, who was sleeping in hers too, she wasn't going to be able to open her eye, not properly, on account of a bite when she woke up. Fleas – or something worse! Didn't look the sort to have something worse, *quite*, and if they had, surely to goodness the General wouldn't have put them in here! Sleeping in their vests meant no luggage. Glancing around the room, Nellie sow none, only a half-unrolled bathing bundle on the dressing-table. Come unbeknownst all right, but where from? out of a ditch and she shouldn't wonder – but what were they doing, children of that age, wandering about at night she'd like to know?

Going round to the side of the bed, Nellie picked up Atalanta's clothes from the floor – what a place to put them to be sure! The frock was dirty and crumpled, but it was good linen and the embroidery was ever so lovely; *that* didn't come from just anywhere. The petticoat and the rest were good class, though on the grubby side, too. Folding them neatly, she placed the underclothes on a chair and hung the frock over the back. No good hanging it up in the wardrobe if they were just going to get up.

When she went round to the other side of the bed, there was the other child's frock laid on the seat of the armchair. 'Well, I'll be jiggered! – If that isn't a Poor-house frock my name's not Nellie Mumbles!' She hadn't lived just up the road from that place as a kid for nothing, gone to the self-same school, too. 'Don't you go mixin' with *them*,' her mother had said, 'you don't know where they comes from – bad 'omes you can be sure, nor never no 'omes from the start 'cos they never oughter been born. Badness breeds badness, an' bad 'omes breeds badness and dirt an' nasty 'abits. They shouldn't go with other kids; 'taint right.'

Stooping, Nellie picked up the frock gingerly between finger and thumb. No mistake about *that*! No wonder there were bites! Dropping it on the back of the chair, she looked at the underclothes that had been beneath it. That petticoat and those drawers had never come out of the Poor-house! But those stockings looked as if they had : matted wool, the heels so full of darns there was no stocking left. Replacing the frock, Nellie's eyes focused on the boots; they weren't the kind a girl with those underclothes would be wanting to wear in the summer – or ever. Lifting one, Nellie turned it over. *W* was hammered into the heel with nails – *W* for *Workhouse*, she'd thought as much. Putting it down, she picked up the sun-bonnet lying beside them : cheap alpaca like the frock, only sand-coloured instead of grey. Well, she knew where *that* belonged. She dropped it where it had been.

Tiptoeing to the side of the bed again, Nellie took another look at Pansy. Any child could have a dirty face and a bunged-up eye, she wasn't such a simpleton as to be taken in by them, and it was her belief that this kid didn't come from the Workhouse, or if she did, she didn't ought to. That snood was good corded ribbon too, not the ribbon they'd dish out to a pauper. But the boots were and that frock and bonnet; no mistaking those boots. It was proper flummoxing and that was a fact. Looking round the room again for any clue in the shape of a bag or something that could help her, Nellie's eyes fell again on the bathing-bundle on the dressing-table. Very quietly, she went over to look at it as if that might tell her something. It told her that if the towel hadn't been dragging on the ground then one of them had laid it there and rolled on it. And when she picked a flap of it aside, she found worse; she found a book whose cover had come off red on the towel and no wonder seeing that the bathing-dress was still damp. Well, really, what a thing to do, and what a place to put a damp messy bundle like that – on the dressing-table if you please. *The Wide Wide World* – wide world or not, the harm was done now, Re-rolling the lot, she carried it over to the chamber cupboard and put it down on the marble top.

No wiser, Nellie woke Pansy first. Talking would show; she could tell then straightaways if the child was a proper little pauper or not. After saying, 'Good morning, miss,' loudly and neither of them blinking so much as an eyelash, she put her hand on Pansy's shoulder. 'Wake up, miss, it's time to get up.'

Pansy opened her eyes and stared at Nellie muzzily.

'I've brought you some water and breakfast is at at nine. Have you any luggage, miss?'

Pansy's brain had cleared enough to feel she ought to have some, that this tall fat maid in the mob-cap expected it.

'No, we're travelling incognito,' said Atalanta's deep voice.

'Incognito, whatever *that* meant! – They 'aven't so much as a comb between the two of them,' Nellie said in the kitchen when she went downstairs. She'd fetched them the visitors' comb from the downstairs lavatory. There was no time to clean the sand-shoes and dry them before nine and as for those boots, they could stay as they were with no boot boy on Sunday and all – not that cleaning would help them much. She'd put them in the dust-bin if she had her way. She was still flummoxed. All the other child had done was to mumble. 'Thank you,' into the bed-clothes which she'd pulled up round her neck. 'Ashamed to be seen sleeping in 'er vest and small wonder. Not the other; she didn't mind a brass farthing. Couldn't tell nothing except the kid's been taught manners, I reckon, and I don't fancy they're Poor-'ouse manners, so what's she doing in those things beats me!' It beat Maud the cook, and Harriet the housemaid, too. Aggie, the kitchen-maid, was peeling potatoes in the scullery and no one consulted her.

Upstairs, in the spare room, things hadn't been going too well. Atalanta had trodden on her spectacles and the glass meant for the right eye had fallen out. What with her bites and the one on her eye and having to put on those clothes again, Pansy felt almost sick. Putting them on in the excitement of a dangerous adventure in the tent with Leah had been one thing; putting them on in cold blood in the morning was quite another. Not that her blood was really cold; being under those blankets had made her absolutely boiling. Being boiling made the thought of the stockings positively loathsome.

'Leave them off,' said Atalanta. 'I haven't got any.'

No, Atalanta hadn't, she had only got dirty sand-shoes, but bare legs and sand-shoes were quite different from bare legs and boots. 'Do you mean to tell me you went down to breakfast with a general in boots with no stockings, on Sunday of all days?' Pansy could *hear* Nana saying it. It wasn't only that which made her put the stockings on though: her feet were so sore she couldn't bear the boots rubbing them raw. On the heel of one she found the *W*. Whatever did it mean? Then she knew; it was for *Workhouse*. She found one on the other boot, too. Fancy not having seen them before! 'Guess what I've found on the heels of Leah's boots!' she said.

Atalanta wouldn't guess.

Pansy told her whether she wanted to know or not. When she looked in the glass, she *did* look awful.

'Evil,' Atalanta said, looking over her shoulder. 'It's your eye that does it, having them different sizes.'

Evil? Pansy looked harder; yes, she did. 'I won't go down to breakfast; I'll start walking home.'

'And cause another disturbance?' Atalanta was trying to force her foot into a sand-shoe without unlacing it. 'Don't be so egocentric,' she said.

'I shan't ask what *egocentric* means,' thought Pansy defiantly.

Atalanta had won against her shoe but she'd split the back. 'You don't suppose a general who's been under fire is going to bother about your eyes not being the same size, do you?'

Pansy shrugged; shrugging, when she remembered it, made her feel older and better. 'You look absolutely – atrocious, blinking through a hole with all those bites round your neck.'

'I expect I do,' Atalanta agreed complacently. 'Faces aren't everything, my father says. He gets cross because my mother makes such a fuss about hers and puts things on it.'

'What things?'

'Oh, ointments and lotions and milk and things – she washes it in milk, and once she went to bed with meat on it.'

'*Meat?*'

'Steak; it feeds it,' said Atalanta indifferently.

Pansy laughed and laughed. She was still laughing when, far away, like the booming of a gun at sea, they heard the breakfast-gong.

Nellie came to show them the way to the dining-room. 'I've got a bite on my eye,' Pansy explained to her. And when she went below, Nellie said to Maud, 'She's not from the Poor-'ouse, boots or no boots.'

The General was already in the dining-room. Pansy's eye would be as right as made no odds by bedtime, he said, but Atalanta's spectacle glass was more serious. He had to go to Crackingbourne tomorrow morning and if she liked he would take her spectacles to a shop there to be repaired and they could be posted to her at Longspit. When Atalanta told him they were going home on Saturday, he decided that she had better hang on to them in case the post missed her.

There was coffee in a percolator, and ham and scrambled eggs and hot rolls wrapped in a white napkin for breakfast.

The General was going to church. He read the lessons and collected the offertory. He didn't think that Atalanta and Pansy would wish to go in their present state of affairs, and he was sending them back to Longspit in the trap with Hamble, his groom, he told them. 'If your grandmother has got back, Atalanta, she is sure to be worrying as to why you haven't turned up, and the sooner you are both delivered the better. Some day I hope to have a telephone, but in this case I have no doubt it would be useless as Chubb's farm won't have one, and neither has Pussyfoot's rectory.'

'It's quite all right, Nonna never worries,' said Atalanta composedly. 'She says it's a waste of time.'

'She might worry about me as I don't belong to her,' Pansy suggested, 'like me worrying about Leah's clothes when I never do about my own. I've made an awful snag in the back of the frock.'

'Yes, I'm afraid Leah's clothes have been a great anxiety to you.' The General's eyes twinkled. 'I see you have the stockings on this morning; it seems the safest place.'

'It's a dreadful place, they tickle like mad.'

'I am afraid we have been a great inconvenience to you.' Atalanta's deep voice sounded courteous. She sounded better than she looked. 'I haven't put myself out for you in any way,' the General said cheerfully. 'I'm not even going to drive you back. Hamble is going to do that.'

'But we had a midnight feast,' Pansy reminded him, 'and we are having breakfast now and we slept in your spare room.'

'At no inconvenience to me. Help yourself to coffee; you know how you like it.'

Pansy, who hardly ever had it, wasn't sure how she did.

'My father likes it black without sugar. He drinks buckets of it, helps to keep him awake to write,' Atalanta said.

'Does he?' Pansy stared at her, seeing and not seeing her father drinking drowsily out of a bucket of coffee, her mother lying with meat on her face. Oh, she did *wish* Atalanta would ask her to come to stay in London.

After breakfast they went to the kitchen garden. In the

morning sun it looked peaceful and very safe. Pansy went to stand between the rows of sweet peas where she had stood in the night and seen what she thought was Long Nose up there on the edge of the field. She tried to feel how frightened she had been, but now that she knew it had been the Vicar and it was broad daylight she couldn't manage to be terrified.

The General picked some apricots, plums and peaches. The apricots and peaches were netted, but the plums were in little muslin bags. He put an assortment in a strawberry basket and handed them to Atalanta. 'Iron rations for the journey,' he said.

Nodding to show that she knew what he was talking about, Atalanta thanked him.

Pansy went further. 'Iron rations must only be eaten in an emergency,' she said, airing her knowledge. Grandfather had explained about them one day when they were sitting on the seat in the garden pretending it was a raft.

'Exactly,' the General said. 'If the horse and trap go over the hedge and you and Hamble are thrown in the ditch, you can each eat an apricot then.'

The church bells had begun to ring. They could hear them floating over from the village. They were ringing *All things bright and beautiful.*

Suddenly Pansy remembered what the General had said. Was Hamble the one that was in the Crimea and lost his hand?

Yes he was.

Now there was a great deal she wanted to ask; she opened her mouth to begin, but Atalanta cut in first, 'The Crimean War ended in eighteen fifty-six, that's –' she scarcely paused she was so good at arithmetic – 'fifty-four years ago. Even if he was only twenty then, he must be seventy-four now – quite old,' she finished casually.

'He's seventy-eight as a matter of fact,' the General said, 'so he must have been twenty-four in fifty-six but he was wounded in fifty-four so he didn't serve throughout the war.'

Pansy didn't mind so much about the dates; she wanted

to know if Florence Nightingale had nursed him. When she questioned the General about this he said, 'Ask him.'

The trap was waiting in front of the terrace. Hamble was there; he had on a blue suit and a bowler hat. Close to, Pansy saw that he had got a hook.

When the good-byes had been said, the General, who had fetched his hat and stick, set off for church by a short cut through the garden and a field, and the trap set out for Longspit.

Pansy had had a good look at the hook before they got into the trap, but she couldn't help shooting glances at it still. She wanted to ask Hamble about Florence Nightingale frightfully, but she didn't know how to begin.

Atalanta broke the ice. 'What did you think of Russia? The General told us you were out in the Crimea.' It did not

sound much more exciting said like that, than if Hamble
had been out to tea.

'What did I think of Russia?' Hamble paused.

'I believe,' thought Pansy, 'he wants to spit and he can't
because of us.'

'T'wouldn't be fit to tell 'ee, miss.'

'Nonsense,' said Atalanta.

'Did Florence Nightingale nurse you?' Pansy burst out.

'Ah – she was a great 'un, but t'were done afore she
come.'

'What was? Do you mean –' Pansy wanted to say 'before
your hand was cut off,' but she hesitated to mention it.

Tapping his hook with his good hand, Hamble said, 'Fust
it went black.'

'*Black?*' said Pansy.

'Aye, black; then they 'acked it off without no chloroform
nor nothin'.'

'Did you watch?' Atalanta inquired.

'I saw 'em – a chopper an' a saw they 'ad, just like 'ackin'
meat.'

Pansy gaped, dumb with horror, and because too there
was so much she wanted to know she didn't know where to
start. 'Did – did it hurt *awfully*?'

''Urt? Streuth!'

'Yes, it must have been excruciating,' Atalanta agreed. 'I
wonder you didn't die.' It sounded rather as though she
thought he should have.

'I'd be under the ground now if it weren't for 'er.'

'Do you mean Florence?' Atalanta asked. 'You said it
happened before she came.'

'So it did, the 'ackin' an' the sawin', but I was mighty ill
after and I reckons without 'er we'd 'ave died in our
thousands instead of 'undreds.'

The Crimea provided them with conversation for a long
time. Hamble told them about the cold, the dreadful icy
winds, and about the mud. The cold had been past believ-
ing, Hamble said. Pansy tried to believe it. Wrapping her
arms round her chest, shutting her eyes, she tried to feel the
cold freezing the very marrow in her bones. It wasn't very

easy with the August sun beating down on her, but she did her best.

Presently, Atalanta asked Hamble what the General's surname was as they would naturally want to write and thank him.

'Naturally,' Pansy said. 'His Christian name is Wellington; he was called after Wellington,' she added, but this was news to no one; she had already told Atalanta and Hamble of course knew.

'General Lancaster-Bruce,' Hamble said. He said it was quite a mouthful. Pansy quite saw that it was, especially with Wellington as well.

'He's a V.C.,' Hamble added.

Pansy gasped. 'A *V.C.*?' She could hardly believe her ears.

'What did he get it for?' Atalanta inquired.

'In India 'twas – not that 'ed tell you mind, but I've 'eard say as 'ow 'e routed a 'ole body of tribesmen up in them 'ills single 'anded, and they be rare savage they be.'

'How?' Atalanta persisted.

'Got be'ind a rock and fired down at the devils. Never seen a finer shot I 'aven't not when it comes to pheasant.'

'I do wish I'd known,' said Pansy.

'What would you have done?' Atalanta demanded.

'Talked to him about it.'

'He wouldn't have talked; you've heard what Hamble's just said.'

'He might have to me,' Pansy thought. Aloud, she said, 'He said a terrier would catch nine times the rats a St. Bernard would.'

'What's that got to do with it?'

Pansy had flushed at the memory of what it had got to do with it, how he had guessed she was surprised he was a general because he was so small, and all the time he was a V.C. 'He said it because he was small.'

'Your face is brick red.'

'I'm hot.' Pansy puffed up some breath over it. She admired the General so much she could hardly bear it. 'I've never seen a V.C. before – at least if I have I haven't known about it, like not knowing when I saw him. We shall have to write it after his name on the envelope – bags I write it!'

'It takes an 'ole line, 'is name and decorations do,' said Hamble, 'Major-General Sir Wellington Lancaster-Bruce, K.C.M.G., V.C., D.S.O.'

'Oh –' Pansy's face, which had been cooling off, got brick red again. If only she had known, she could have been different. But *he* hadn't been. She saw him sitting at the kitchen table carefully pulling the little skewered onion out of the bottle. He hadn't seemed as though he wanted to be different. Thinking about the little onion comforted her a great deal. Then her eye fell on the basket of iron rations and she felt better still. She felt so much better that, although they weren't in the ditch, she decided to offer Hamble an apricot.

Hamble didn't want an apricot, or a plum, or a peach; he preferred to smoke. Hooking the reins round his hook, he pulled out his pipe and tobacco-pouch from his pocket and packing his pipe, pulled out a box of matches and lit it, all with one hand. Pansy longed to offer to hold the reins while all this was going on, but was afraid it might offend him.

It was shorter by road to Longspit than by cliff, and they reached it in just over two hours. In the lane they very nearly ran over Nonna, who suddenly came out of the gate leading to the high part of the downs. When Pansy cried, 'It's us!' Nonna said, 'Oh, *there* you are! I was just beginning to wonder where you were. I've been on the downs looking for two specks coming along the cliff.' Only *beginning* to wonder, thought Pansy with delight. The Aunts and Nana would have been in a frenzy by now.

'Good morning,' Nonna smiled up at Hamble as though she was a great friend of his which of course she wasn't. 'This is kind of you.'

'Good morning, ma'am,' Hamble, who had taken his pipe out of his mouth, touched his bowler with his hook.

'We spent the night – part of it – with a V.C.!' Pansy cried, 'and the other part on a stack!'

'How delicious, darling! – You must tell me all about it.' It was hardly worth getting up into the trap with such a few yards to go, Nonna said, so while the horse walked slowly she walked behind, calling out her news and asking for theirs in her carrying trailing voice.

She had got back about an hour or so ago. The Bishop, who had been spending the night with Pussy – Nonna called him 'Pussy' too – 'not our Bishop, the Bishop of this diocese,' she explained, had driven off very early to take the communion service at Stone Abbas and had kindly taken her with him. After breakfasting in the Vicarage, they had come on to Font Abbas, a mile away from here, where the Bishop was preaching at Matins, and he had most generously sent her back in his carriage. 'Now tell me everything about yourselves,' she called gaily. How could they tell her everything now? Pansy thought; she didn't even know where to begin. But Atalanta tied up the news in a neat little parcel and threw it down to Nonna as though it were no more exciting than a parcel of fish. 'We missed the train and walked along the cliff. We stayed the night with General Wellington Lancaster-Bruce at Spettiscombe and he sent us back in his trap.'

'There's more, there's more!' Pansy shrieked inside her, but all she cried was 'Is Leah in the cupboard?'

'Not now,' said Nonna, 'and she's never going to be again; no one is. We went round there, Pussy and I, and caught him at it red-handed.' Pansy saw Nonna and Pussy clutching hold of Long Nose who was pushing Leah into the cupboard, his hands in scarlet gloves.

'There's going to be an inquiry and he'll be dismissed and that Matron with him – Pussy and the Bishop will see to that,' Nonna explained. 'Leah's at the Rectory now. She's quite safe; the Pussies have taken her under their wing.'

15

SUNDAY, MONDAY, CURRANTS
AND A PLAN

THE good news of Leah's rescue, that no one was ever going
to be put into the cupboard again, and Long Nose and
Matron were going to be sent away, filled Pansy with
happiness as, up in the bedroom at the farm, she began to
take off Leah's clothes. With her bare feet on the cool lino-
leum, she pulled the horrible frock over her head and
dropped it on the floor. 'I shall never have to put it on again
as long as I live,' she thought, 'or the stockings or the boots
or the bonnet. But Leah – Leah will have to, if she doesn't
stay with the Pussies for ever.' Nonna hadn't said that she
would, and in the excitement of everything and the longing
to undress, Pansy hadn't asked. At least Leah wouldn't be
sent back to the Workhouse while Long Nose and Matron
were still there; the Pussies wouldn't let her go; she was
under their wing and she was safe. But afterwards – when
the new Master and Matron came, would she have to go
back then? 'I should like to throw the clothes away,' Pansy
thought, giving the frock a shove with her foot, 'but it
wouldn't help. If she does have to go back and hasn't got
her clothes, they'll only be cross and give her some more.'

Back in one of her own frocks again, Pansy felt absolutely
different. She was going to feel even better when she had
bathed.

'I should think if there are any harvesters still on you,'
Nonna had said, 'they must all be gorged by now and quite
somnolent, so that if you do plunge into the sea they'll
certainly be taken by surprise and be too fat and sleepy to
swim. Put your whole head under by all means, but it

would be a good thing if you could get your hair to stop dripping before we go to church this evening.'

Dripping, dripping, dripping – what an extraordinary Sunday it was being, Pansy thought happily.

There was a lovely Sunday dinner – duck and green peas and potatoes and cherry tart and a bowl of cream with a yellow crust on the top. It was unnecessary for Pansy to eat nine potatoes because in the end she hadn't missed a meal at all. She had had tea with the herbalist and supper and breakfast with the General. Fishing about in the big china vegetable-dish, she saw at once that she couldn't possibly have eaten nine, even if she *had* missed three meals. If all the potatoes had been the size of marbles, she could have, but there were only two tiny ones.

When they were all settled and Mrs Chubb had flapped a bluebottle out of the window with the oven-cloth and gone back to the kitchen, Pansy said, 'Will Leah stay with the Pussies always? She won't have to go back to the Work-house, will she, Nonna?'

'I don't know, darling. I don't think she can very well remain at the Rectory indefinitely,' Nonna said. 'But she certainly won't go back till that horrible man and woman have gone – it would be like throwing her to the sharks.'

'*Couldn't* the Pussies keep her?'

'I am afraid not. She's only a child and they're an elderly couple, and their maids who have been with them for years are old too. If Leah were fourteen, it would be different. She could go into service,' Nonna explained, 'in some nice house where they would be kind to her.'

'She won't be fourteen for three years. Do you think,' said Pansy thoughtfully, 'she could pretend to be fourteen?'

'No, I'm quite sure she couldn't. And I am equally sure,' said Nonna, 'that if she came to live with me Dorcas would leave immediately and then Dorcas would have no home.'

'Suppose she came to us?' Pansy suggested eagerly. 'Do you think Aunt Susu and Aunt Katie would have her? I'm sure Grandfather would arrange something.'

Nonna seemed doubtful. 'Besides, I'm not at all sure that Leah would be happy if she was completely uprooted and transplanted away from the kind of companionship she has been accustomed to. She might feel that she was neither fish nor fowl nor good red herring. If the Workhouse is run properly and she has friends among the children there –' Nonna's voice trailed into silence and Pansy saw that she was frowning. Then her face cleared; she smiled and said, 'Stop worrying, Pansy. Leah's in clover at the moment, and I dare say something will work out perfectly in the end.'

'I wonder what she's doing now?' Pansy forked up a lovely bit of crisp duck's skin.

'The same as we are,' said Atalanta, 'and if she's got any sense she'll eat everything she can lay her hands on.' Atalanta wasn't doing too badly herself. Slowly and methodically she was stuffing her fork with peas. Three prongs were full and she had started on the fourth. It was big, even for a meat fork. She couldn't have done it with a smaller one, thought Pansy admiringly, the peas would have been too close. As she watched, Atalanta spiked the last two on and put the whole lot in her mouth without even saying 'Look what I've done!'

'The poor little thing looked as if she could do with some food,' Nonna said.

'I do wish I could watch her eating,' Pansy sighed.

'What on earth for? If she was a pitcher-plant in the jungle eating flies, there might be some point in it.' Atalanta's deep voice was gruff with peas.

'Pansy, quite naturally, wants to see the end of the story – not that it's the end; I hope Leah will live happily to be a hundred, if she'd like that – but it's the end of Pansy's bit of the story.' Nonna said.

'Couldn't we go to Crackingbourne and see her? I know there's no train there and back on the same day, but supposing Mr Chubb had to go, couldn't we go with him?' Pansy urged.

'He only goes on market day, which is Saturday, you know, he said so.' Atalanta's voice was clear of peas.

'Wishful thinking –' Nonna had her dreaming look as though she were thinking about a painting.

Atalanta didn't go down to bathe that afternoon. She

said she was sure the harvesters had gone of their own accord. She lay flat on her back on the grass under the mountain-ash and slept. Pansy went down to the sea alone. Nonna, who had gone off to paint, didn't seem to mind a bit if she drowned; it was gorgeous. It seemed rather a fag to blow up her wings to bathe by herself, so she decided to go into the deepest pool, which didn't count as the sea, to begin with. It was better for plunging too. After the heat outside the water was frightfully cold; going in quickly was awful. The water came up to her chest. She stopped for a moment, just standing there, gasping. If she was going to put her whole head under there wasn't much need to hurry, she thought; the harvesters would drown anyway. She squinted down at her neck to see if they were hopping up to dry ground, but couldn't see any. Then she pinched her nose, and scrunched down on her heels till she felt the water closing over her head. She had unplaited her hair to let out the harvesters, and when she came up, bursting for breath, it was all over her face like seaweed clinging to a post. Picking it away, she felt brave and clean and splendid. She looked for the gorged somnolent harvester bodies, feeling cruel and sorry for them, but as there were none, she went back to hating them.

It was the next day, on Monday, that Mrs Chubb said the thing that mattered. She said it while she was picking blackcurrants from one of the bushes covered with lace curtains. Pansy started the conversation that led up to it; 'In the moonlight, these bushes must look like ghosts,' she said, 'crouching ghosts. Atalanta and I can't see them from our bedroom, of course.' She was rather glad they couldn't.

'That's right,' agreed Mrs Chubb cheerfully, 'but we 'as to 'ave summat, the birds are that greedy you wouldn't credit. Seein' as you mention ghosts, if you was to 'ear a noise tomorrow night – leastways early Wednesday mornin' – don't go gettin' no fearsome notions about ghosts into yer 'ead as there won't be no need.'

'What noises?'

'Pitter-pat, pitter-pat.'

'*Footsteps?*' In spite of the hot sun and what Mrs Chubb said about not having fearsome notions, Pansy felt a cold tremor deep inside her.

'Scores of little trottin' 'ooves.' Bent over the currants, when Mrs Chubb lifted her smiling face it was on a level with Pansy's. Pansy had never seen it so close before, and she saw that Mrs Chubb's eyebrows, which were fair and quite thick for a little way, suddenly stopped altogether like a grass track.

'Trotting ghosts?' Pansy laughed.

'Sheep, not ghosts, going to the sheep fair at Cracking-bourne. Job 'Awkins, from t'other side o' Golden Down, 'e allus starts wi' 'is sheep one in the mornin' an' passes 'ere round cock crow. 'E stops off at Dobson's meadow to rest 'em and goes on in the evenin' to 'is brother's farm near Crackingbourne for the night. Will now, 'im an' Alf don't start till midday an' they goes straight on to Penn's farm, three mile this side o' Crackingbourne an' bides the night an' goes on in the mornin' same as Job do.'

While Pansy listened, she had had a great idea. Will was Mr Chubb and Alf the shepherd, and they were going to the sheep fair. 'I want to go to Crackingbourne just dread-fully – to see Leah. Could I go with Mr Chubb and Alf?'

'You!' Mrs Chubb laughed, 'Walk all that way! You'd be smothered in dust from 'ead to foot by the time you got there – if you ever did! You wouldn't credit the dust them sheep kicks up an' all.'

'I wouldn't mind.'

'Well, Will wouldn't take you not if it was ever so, but I tells you wot –' Mrs Chubb, who had just draped the bush in the curtain again, stood up – 'I'll be takin' the gig to Crackingbourne Thursday evenin' to fetch Will an' Alf back, an' p'raps you could come along with me.'

'Oh yes, *please*! How simply lovely!' cried Pansy.

'It's not for me to say wot you can and can't do, mind, and now I comes to think of it –' Mrs Chubb had stopped smiling, 'I think p'raps it mightn't do after all.'

'Why?' Why ever shouldn't it? thought Pansy in dismay.

'Well, it's like this – they wouldn't want fetchin' till quite

latish, round about dark, an' I couldn't get there afore, not
if they wanted it. Wot with the milkin' an' a score o' t'other
things – an' there'll be cold supper that night if madam
don't mind, an' I shan't be stoppin' there not more than just
long enough to pick 'em up, see? I can't be awaitin' more
than five minutes.'

'I could see Leah in five minutes.'

'But you wouldn't be done in five minutes or my name's
not Polly Chubb.'

'I would, I promise. Besides, Dobbin will want a rest after
all that way,' Pansy pointed out triumphantly.

'No, 'e won't, an' it's no manner o' good an, argufyin'.'
Mrs Chubb lifted up the curtain from the next bush.
'Twenty minutes is all I could give you.'

'Twenty! – oh, thanks *awfully*!' Pansy beamed with
delight.

'Though wot you wants to go for, I dunno. Best leave the poor mite alone now to them wot's got 'er. If I was madam I don't know as I'd let you go and come back when you oughter be in bed.'

'No, I oughtn't! And *you'd* want to see Leah. If you'd seen Long Nose and Matron, you'd want to see how she was now she's escaped.'

'If I'd seen them varmints I'd 'ave given 'em a piece o' my mind.'

Varmints, thought Pansy delightedly. What a pity Mrs Chubb hadn't seen them. She had heard her giving a piece of her mind to the cock the other day for pecking the lettuces, and she bet she'd have given an even better piece to Long Nose and Matron, if she hadn't been frightened. 'I wish you *had* seen them.'

'Now don't go bankin' on comin'.' Mrs Chubb was picking off strings of currants very quickly. 'It don't never do to count yer chickens afore they're 'atched, an' if madam don't allow it there's no more to be said.'

'She will!' Pansy assured her eagerly. 'She never minds anything. She says the whole thing about a holiday is to do something different from usual. I'll go and ask her!'

Nonna was easier to find than usual. She was sitting with her embroidery in the big squashy rattan chair under the walnut tree embroidering plums on the hem of a petticoat. 'But no one will see them unless it hangs down,' Pansy had pointed out yesterday, and Nonna had said, '*I* shall know they are there.' Now she told Pansy of course she could go to Crackingbourne. 'But twenty minutes doesn't seem very long, yet it certainly wouldn't be fair to keep Mrs Chubb waiting. Why not bring Leah back with you?'

Pansy could hardly believe that Nonna had really said that as casually as if it were something quite ordinary – like brining back some bullseyes from the village shop. '*Can I?*'

'I don't see why not. I'm sure Mrs Chubb will be able to find somewhere for her to sleep, and it will be a bit of an outing for her and I'm certain the Pussies won't mind.' Nonna stuck her needle into the middle of a golden plum, 'I ought to have brought another skein of silk.'

'How long can she stay?' Pansy asked eagerly.

'Till we can get her back, I suppose,' Nonna said vaguely.

Pansy thought about the trains. There was one to Crackingbourne at seven-thirty on Friday morning and not another till Monday. They went on Mondays, Wednesdays, and Fridays. They came back on Tuesdays, Thursdays, and Saturday evenings. There was no train on Sunday. If Leah went back on the Friday train she would only have the night, when she would be asleep, and an early breakfast. If she stayed till Monday, *they* would have gone – Nonna and Atalanta and Pansy on Saturday morning.

'Why can't she go back in the gig with Chubb on Saturday when he goes to market?' Nonna said as if she were asking a question.

'She can!' Pansy answered, and that settled everything.

16

PITTER-PAT, PUSSY AND LEAH

PANSY dreamt she was playing cricket. She was batting and the Workhouse children were fielding. She was just looking for Leah when she saw that Long Nose was going to bowl. He had taken off his coat. Charging down towards her in his shirt and waistcoat and trousers, he flung his arm over. He wasn't just trying to bowl, he was trying to kill her. The ball came hurtling straight at her, whizzing past, it hit the stumps with a crack and the bails shot straight up into the sky. 'How's that?' Long Nose shouted.

'Out!' cried a high-pitched voice, 'Out!-Out!-Out!' It was Willie Stacey the herbalist. He was umpiring, with his pink chest showing and his shirtfront tied around his waist like an apron.

Pansy woke up then. She was very glad to find it had been a dream; with Long Nose trying to kill her it had been so horrible. She was very glad too to find that it was greyish daylight and not dark. Then she realized that the 'Out!-Out!-Out! was still going on. How could it be if it was a dream? And then she heard something else, a kind of tapping, a pitter-patting – the *sheep*! It wasn't Willie Stacey calling 'Out', it was the sheepdog barking.

Getting out of bed, she went over to the window and looked out. They were going along the lane. She couldn't see them because of the hedge, and it wasn't light enough to have seen much if the hedge hadn't been there, but she could imagine them quite well, pattering along, shoving each other, as she had seen them being driven to the cattle market at home. It was the early morning of tomorrow, tomorrow was today, the day when she was going to Crackingbourne to fetch Leah! She was awake, but her dream was still with her; with a tremor of fear she imagined Long Nose hurtling in at the door to bowl at her. Running back, she scuttled into bed and lay there listening till the faraway barking didn't sound like 'Out' any more.

This time tomorrow Leah would be sleeping in the attic. Lying awake, Pansy remembered again how absolutely gorgeous it was up there, with the sloping ceiling with a skylight, and the little window, and water trickling in the tank. 'This is where our Charlie used to sleep,' Mrs Chubb had told her. 'Wi' eight of 'em, it was a bit of a squeeze and that's a fact.' Pansy, who had known already about Mrs Chubb's eight children, seven daughters and one son – Lucy, Rosie, Connie, Ethel, Mab. Ivy, Daisy and Charlie – hadn't wanted to discuss them just then; she had been too interested in the enormous feather mattress, humped up in the middle and splaying over the floor. Was Leah going to sleep on that? Before she had had time to ask, Mrs Chubb had said, 'That's our feather bed – Will's an' mine. I puts it up 'ere come summer. We don't never sleep on it in the 'eat, we'd suff'cate.'

'I slept on a feather bed once when I stayed away. It was scrumptious fun. I didn't suffocate, but it was in October,' Pansy had explained, and then she had asked if Leah was going to sleep on it. 'Won't she suffocate?'

'I 'spects she would if she did!' Mrs Chubb had laughed. Stooping, she had leant across the feather bed and tugged it towards her till the whole lot was on the floor. Pansy saw then what the hump had been; it was a camp-bed. She had helped Mrs Chubb tug the feather bed into the corner by the water-tank. After that, she had leant out of the window and watched one of the fantails waddling down the old tiles of the roof. She had envied Leah, because she was going to sleep in the attic, so much that she could hardly bear it.

It was a good thing Atalanta didn't want to go to Crackingbourne because the gig was going to be stuffed on the way back. 'Why on earth should I *want* to go?' Atalanta had asked. There were so many reasons why she should that for a moment Pansy had been flummoxed as to which of them to say. 'To see Leah in my frock.' It was silly to have said that because Atalanta had seen Leah in it already, and if Leah was coming to stay wearing it, Atalanta would see her in it again.

Going over all this in her mind now, longing to see Leah, Pansy could hardly wait for the evening, but while she was counting the hours to it, she fell asleep again.

The day did not go so slowly after all. They went down to the beach in the morning, Pansy and Atalanta and Nonna. Nonna paddled. She stood in the middle of a shallow pool, shading her green grass hat with a faded green parasol, and gazed out to sea. 'I would give ten years of my life to be able to paint water,' she murmured dreamily.

Ten years! thought Pansy. Ten years was the whole of her own life. When she thought of some of the lovely things she had done since she was born and how awful it would have been to have missed them, she couldn't believe that Nonna could really mean what she said. 'Would you really, Nonna? – honest Injun?'

'Honest Injun?' Nonna paused to consider. 'No, I suppose not really.' Sitting down at the side of the pool, she dabbled her fingers in a little basin that looked as if it had been scooped out of the rock with a spoon. The water went over her rings, drowning the diamonds and sapphires and rubies, but she didn't seem to mind.

Seven hours and a bit after Nonna put her fingers in the pool, Pansy was getting down from the gig outside Saint John's Rectory in Crackingbourne. 'Careful,' said Mrs Chubb. 'I'll be waitin' 'ere and don't be no longer than you can 'elp, there's a good girl.'

No, Pansy wouldn't. Leah ought to be ready and waiting. Nonna had written to tell the Pussies about everything.

The Rectory gate was open. There was only a little bit of front garden and in the gathering darkness Pansy saw a big round bed with some geraniums and straggling nasturtiums. When she had rung the front door bell, she looked back at Mrs Chubb; the gig was so high that quite a lot of her showed over the top of the hedge. When Pansy gave a little wave, Mrs Chubb nodded her brown straw hat. Pansy was looking back at the door again when it was opened by an elderly prim-looking maid. Nonna had been right; she was too old to be fun for Leah. Pansy could see that. Pansy went straight to the point, 'Please I've come for Leah.'

The maid smiled a little which made her look more friendly. 'Come in, miss, we're expecting you.' She stood aside for Pansy to go into the lighted hall.

'Whom have we got here?' A clergyman – it must be Pussy – was coming down the hall.

'It's the child for Leah, sir.'

'Ah – come in, my dear. Leah? Where is Leah, Emily?'

'I'll find her, sir.'

Putting a hand on Pansy's shoulder, Pussy guided her down the hall. He wasn't the least bit like a cat. It was only because of his name that he was called 'Pussy', of course, but just the same she had rather expected him to be like one. His face was red with tufts of white hair growing on his cheeks.

'Are you the one who swapped places with Leah?' he asked.

'Yes.'

'Well, you did a good day's work helping to expose that tyrant – a couple of them.'

Pansy felt very pleased. 'It was my good deed,' she thought, and then remembered that she had forgotten about today's; but she hadn't time to worry about that just now.

'My wife will be sorry to miss you,' Pussy went on, 'but she had to go straight from the jumble-sale to a meeting, I'm afraid.' He stopped at the end of the hall where an open door led into the garden. 'Leah!' he called. 'I don't expect she's still out there though that's where she usually is. Leah!' he called again, and letting go of Pansy's shoulder went out on to the lawn.

Following, Pansy peered down the long, overgrown garden. There seemed to be a shrubbery at the end; perhaps Leah was there? No, she ought to be waiting, *ready*. Turning to look at the house, she saw Leah coming down the hall. 'Here she is!' Pansy cried. She took a step towards the

house and then stopped for a moment, gaping. When you have been seeing someone for five days with your mind's eye dressed in your own blue and white striped frock, it is bound to come as a surprise to see them in a yellow smock with little pink roses all over it. Leah's straw hat wasn't Pansy's, and she had on black cotton stockings and black button shoes which weren't Pansy's either. On one arm she carried a blue coat and in her other hand a canvas bag and Pansy's hat.

Pussy's voice saying, 'Here you are, all neat and trim,' helped Pansy to recover from her surprise.

'Hullo,' said Pansy.

''Ullo,' Leah grinned. Even before she did that, her face looked different from the face that Pansy had mostly been remembering, although she hadn't forgotten how Leah had smiled that once just before she left the tent.

'You've got a new frock.'

'Yus, miss – leastways 'tis an' 'taint like. Missus Pussyfoot, 'er says, Leah, 'er says, there's summat in jumble reel nice wot'll do for yer.'

'It's awfully nice.' Pansy gazed admiringly.

'I've got yer frock an' purse an' money an' shoes in the bag an' 'ere's yer 'at.' Putting down the bag, Leah held out Pansy's hat.

'Thank you,' Pansy took it. 'You have the money, but I think I'd better have my hat. But wouldn't you like the frock – so that you've got two – and the shoes? I've got quite a lot of frocks and I've bought some more sand-shoes in the village shop.'

'I'm not really sure that the clothes are yours to give away,' Pussy remarked gently. 'I think they should be regarded as a loan, at any rate till you get home.'

Pansy quite saw that he might be right. She told Leah that her things were waiting at the farm. Mrs Chubb had washed the frock and bonnet and stockings and cleaned the boots too. Pansy did not add that Mrs Chubb had also mended the frock and darned the stockings, because she didn't feel that this was the moment to talk about the tear and the hole. She didn't like reminding Leah of those hateful clothes at all, but she had to mention them. While she was talking, Leah had put on the coat. 'It is *brand* new?' Pansy asked. It looked it.

'Jumble,' Leah told her proudly.

'I have a well-to-do parishioner whose daughter is, fortunately for Leah, outgrowing her clothes,' Pussy explained contentedly. 'The jumble is brought here before it goes to the parish hall for the sale, so that my wife was able to fit out Leah. She bought the things of course,' he added as though Pansy were about to object, 'for the price they would have been sold for.'

Leah thrust forward a foot. ' 'Er buyed these 'ere shoes in a shop, an' the stockin's an' that 'at. You'll be 'avin' yers back, 'er said.'

'Have you –' Pansy stopped. She had been going to ask Leah if she still had that awful grey woollen vest and the calico drawers, but with Pussy there she couldn't very well.

'An' that's not all!' said Leah triumphantly. 'You wait till yer see wot's under me dress!'

Oh good! Leah meant new drawers and vest and perhaps a petticoat too; Pansy did hope so.

Putting his hand in his pocket, Pussy brought out a coin and held it out to Leah. 'This is for you – half a crown, to spend as you like, then when you have returned Pansy's money to her which, in spite of her kind offer I think you should, you will both have some money of your own.' Leah stood stock still for a minute staring at him; then she took a quick step forward and eagerly snatched the money. 'Oh, sir, thank you, sir –'

'And now I expect you had better be off,' Pussy said. He went out to the gig with them and talked to Mrs Chubb. As the children climbed into the gig Pansy heard Mrs Chubb say to Pussy, 'Poor little mite – looks as if a good meal 'ud do 'er good. Not but wot you've given 'er good meals that I'll wager, sir,' she hastened to add, 'but them in that Poor-'ouse 'asn't, I'll warrant.'

'They didn't, you're right there,' Pussy agreed. 'There's been a lot of jiggery-pokery going on in that place, but we're on to it now and conditions are going to be very different in future, I trust.'

'I'm glad to 'ear it, sir, I must say.'

When the good-byes were over, Mrs Chubb jerked the reins, told Dobbin to wake up, and they started off for the Shoulder of Mutton to pick up Mr Chubb and Alf, the shepherd.

'I'm countin' on you to 'elp feed the 'ens, Leah,' Mrs Chubb sounded as though she had been waiting for Leah to come and help her with the hens for a long time.

''Ens – not 'arf I won't!' Leah said eagerly.

Mrs Chubb had never asked *her* to, thought Pansy, chagrined, though it wouldn't have been much of a treat because she had often fed Grandfather's, but Mrs Chubb had invited her and Atalanta to tickle the porker with a stick. 'Can I show Leah how to tickle the porker with a stick?' she asked Mrs Chubb.

'Bless you, dearie, o' course you can.'

Mrs Chubb and Leah got on so well together that Pansy began to feel rather left out. 'It was *I* who lent Leah my bathing-dress,' she thought rather crossly, and then Mrs Chubb said, 'Miss Pansy'll take you down and show you the sea. She's a great one for the water, aren't you, luv?,' and although Pansy had only *really* swum for a minute and Leah could swim properly and ought to have been a fish, Pansy felt a good deal better.

When they reached the Shoulder of Mutton, Mrs Chubb said, 'You'd 'ave thought they might 'ave been on the look-out for us, but not a bit of it! Down I'll 'ave to get.'

'Would you like me to go and tell them we're here?' Pansy suggested. She didn't much want to; she felt rather shy. There was a great deal of noise coming from inside the pub, and then suddenly there was a great bellow of laughter.

'No, dearie, I'll go. Sounds the fair 'as gone to their 'eads. It don't 'appen but once a year, thanks be. 'Ere, you take these, there's a good girl –' Mrs Chubb held out the reins to Pansy.

'*Me?*' Pansy could hardly believe it. Getting up, she grabbed them joyfully.

'Jus' 'old 'em, don't go a-tuggin', an' I won't be no more'n a jiffy. Dobbin won't budge – glad to 'ave a snooze.'

When Mrs Chubb had gone, Pansy thought, 'Fancy Leah and me being alone in a gig like this and me holding the reins.' She didn't say it. Standing with her eyes glued to Dobbin's ears, she said, 'Are you glad you came, Leah?'

'Wotcher think?' answered Leah.

Dobbin shook his head once, but otherwise he stayed quite still. Pansy didn't want him to bolt, but she did rather wish he would move again before the others came. When they did come, Mr Chubb was in rattling good form. He chucked Leah under the chin and told her she was a bonnie lass and no mistake, and he slapped Pansy on the back and said he'd as lief have her drive Dobbin as anyone in the country. He took the reins from her all the same, and sat down with a thud in his usual place. Pansy sat between him and Leah, and Mrs Chubb and Alf sat opposite. Trusty, the collie, crawled in under the seat behind Alf's legs.

Mr and Mrs Chubb and Alf talked about the fair. Screwing round sideways to face Leah, Pansy told her about the farm. She didn't tell her about the attic, she wanted it to be a surprise. Then Leah, who had screwed round too, told Pansy about the Pussies and about what had happened at the Workhouse when she got back from the beach that day. Long Nose had just finished beating her, ''e didn't 'arf try an' kill me,' and he was just going to put her in the cupboard 'when the Rector an' Miss At'lanta's gran comed; they comed without no knockin' nor ringin' nor nothin', an' they didn't 'arf give it to Long Nose and Matron 'ot an' strong.'

Pansy, who had never heard Nonna giving anyone anything hot and strong, but knew her blood had been up, listened eagerly. What did she *say*?'

''Er called 'im a n'orrible bully, 'er did. I dunno wot else 'er said, I was beat 'arf silly.'

'Poor Leah,' said Pansy, 'you're safe now.' Crowded into the gig, holding on to the edge of it, revelling in the swaying movement, the clop of hooves and the grinding of the wheels on the road, Pansy thought how safe they were.

It seemed almost a pity that Long Nose wasn't chasing them.

Presently, everyone grew silent. The Chubbs and Alf had said all they wanted to say about the fair, and Pansy and Leah had stopped for the moment too. Dobbin was walking now; the lane was so narrow the branches of the elder bushes, heavy with berries, reached out to brush them. Presently, Mrs Chubb would make the berries into wine.

Trundling slowly through the hot summer darkness, Pansy thought what a long time ago the end of term seemed – ten days ago, counting today which was almost over. Ten good deeds. *Had* she done one today? No, she hadn't. Then, looking back through the day she remembered about the tube of ultramarine paint which Nonna had left on her bed. 'I shall have to go back and get it; I must have it for the sea.' Pansy had said, 'I'll go.' The funny thing was that although they had reached the beginning of the track to the sea, and it was quite a long way back, Pansy had forgotten to think of it as a good deed until now. She had *wanted* to do it for Nonna, it hadn't been only because she knew she ought to. It could count as her good deed surely, even if she hadn't done it purposely for one? Perhaps, she thought, good deeds were like that – presently you stopped doing them on purpose and did them without thinking.

Pansy's fortune had come true, there could be no doubt about it at all, so Nonna had said, but Nonna's and Atalanta's were not quite so obvious, although the sweep *might* be the dark handsome visitor and the Roman coin *might* be riches. They would just have to wait and see if anything else happened, Nonna said.

'How happy I am,' Pansy thought, 'I'm absolutely perfectly happy,' but she had no sooner thought it than something turned up to spoil it. Leah. When a new Master and Matron came to the Workhouse, she would have to go back; she would have to take off her nice new clothes and put on those other awful things and go. '*Sufficient unto the day is the evil thereof,*' Aunt Susu always said. It came out of the Bible and meant you were to live in the present and not worry about the future. It wasn't very easy, especially if you knew there was something horrid waiting for you – like all your sums being wrong, or having a tooth out; and now there was this beastly thing waiting for Leah.

Then suddenly an owl hooted. It was a surprise, but it wasn't terrifying like that sudden hoot when they were on the stack. It reminded Mrs Chubb of the baby owl she had found abandoned in the garden, and which she had reared on little bits of raw meat till it was old enough to fly off and scavenge for itself. The mention of meat reminded Mr Chubb of the time he ate the horse-meat meant for the dogs in mistake for beef. Pansy thought this so funny she laughed hilariously and stopped worrying about Leah.

When Pansy woke up the next morning she was already excited. She remembered at once, why – she was going to show Leah all the animals on the farm and then take her down to the beach to bathe. When she jumped out of bed and ran over to the window to see what kind of a day it was, she saw Leah and Mrs Chubb crossing the midden. She could hardly believe it, she was so cross and disappointed. Now Mrs Chubb would have shown Leah everything. Perhaps it was late and they had waited for her to come and then gone without her? But when Pansy opened the bedroom door and poked her head round to look at the landing clock, she saw it was only twenty-past seven, earlier than she generally got up. Dressing quickly, she rushed downstairs. She found Mrs Chubb and Leah in the dairy and Leah was skimming the cream off a pan of milk. 'Careful does it,' said Mrs Chubb, 'don't go a'diggin' too deep.'

'Have you shown Leah *everything*?' Pansy cried. 'I saw you coming across the midden. Why didn't you wait for me?'

'Lawks-a-mussy, luv, we ain't got time to go a-gawpin' at porker and them dratted gobblers this hour o' the mornin'! All we done was to take some milk to the barn cat. She's 'ad 'er kittens tho' where, I dunno for sure. We never seed naught, but it's my belief she's got 'em back in straw up top, but it don't do to go a-pokin' an' a-pryin' – tho' I reckons we'll know afore the day's out so's you can 'ave a peep afore you goes tomorrer. As to the rest – there's plenty for you to be a-showin' of to Leah so don't go thinkin' no diff'rent, there's a good girl.'

There was so much for Pansy to show Leah after all, so many things to do before and after breakfast, that a good slice of the last morning went by in no time. Nonna said she would get Leah a bathing-dress if there was one to be found in the village shop, but there wasn't. Pansy didn't want to share hers again if she could help it. She wanted to bathe at the same time as Leah. Fortunately, Mrs Chubb came to the rescue. Rummaging in the drawer of the kitchen dresser, she dragged out a blue cotton bathing-dress, left behind, unwanted, by a family of visitors the summer before. It was a bit on the big side, but no bigger than Nonna's was for Atalanta, so that was all right.

'As it's our last day, we'll have picnic lunches,' Nonna had said, 'so that we can all do exactly what we like and be quite untrammelled,' as though they hadn't been late for almost every meal and done exactly as they liked ever since they came. What Nonna liked was to take her picnic to finish a painting of the cornfield. Pansy and Leah and Atalanta took theirs to the beach.

There was plenty of water for Leah to swim in. Watching her, Pansy decided that she swam more like a dog than a fish. When Leah scrambled up on to a rock and plunged in head first, Pansy thought exultantly, 'Now she's washed herself clean of the Workhouse for ever,' – but if she had to go back there, it wouldn't be for ever. She didn't want to think about that now, and it was the unexpected that always happened according to Nana, so if Leah was expected to go back, perhaps she never would. Hurling herself forward on her wings, Pansy tried to swim slowly with great sweeping strokes as Atalanta did. 'What would you like to do if there's some time before tea, Leah?' Pansy asked as they trailed back up the track. 'Would you like to tickle the porker?'

'If you tickle it any more, it will go bald,' Atalanta said.

'No, it won't. You can see a lot of skin – you always could, it's not our fault – that's how the hairs grow, few and far between.' Snatching a long grass, Pansy swished at one of Atalanta's fat bare legs. 'Would you like to, Leah?'

'Naw, miss, I b'aint got no time not for porker. I gotter 'elp Missus Chubb wi' milkin' when I gets back.'

'Watch her, I suppose you mean,' Atalanta said. "Milking's a knack, like ringing church bells.'

'Missus Chubb'll learn me.'

'She'll *teach* and you'll *learn*.' Atalanta sounded like a school-mistress.

Pansy said nothing. At the thought of Mrs Chubb teaching Leah to milk, of Leah going back to do it, of everything being already arranged between the two of them, she felt so left out, so *desolate,* that her eyes filled suddenly with tears. No one saw.

After tea, Nonna wanted Pansy's help. 'Come and help me find a butterfly-orchis, darling. The sexton says they grow in that little wood by the side of the road at the bottom of the downs – only if you want to, of course,' she added.

Atalanta was reading and Leah was milking and Pansy did want to. She would love to find a butterfly-orchis. If they found two, one each, she would take hers home to Grandfather.

On the way, Nonna said, 'I am glad Leah and Mrs Chubb get on so well together. Just think how disappointing it would have been if they hadn't.'

Pansy, who had never imagined Leah and Mrs Chubb disliking each other, quite saw how wretched it would have been if they had. This made her feel better about the milking.

They couldn't find any orchises, but the milking was over when they got back to the farm, and after tickling the porker, Pansy and Leah played touch wood. Then they went with Mr Chubb to find the kittens.

When Nonna started to write a letter after supper, Pansy was shocked. 'It's your last evening.'

'It won't take very long, and I hope it will bear delicious fruit.'

'What fruit?' Pansy asked.

'I'll tell you in the train tomorrow, my darling lamb.'

Tomorrow had come. Pansy stood gazing out of the train window till there was no hope of seeing the sea again, and the downs had given place to flat fields. Slumping down in the corner seat opposite Nonna, she said, 'What fruit?'

'Fruit?' questioned Nonna vaguely.

'The delicious fruit of your letter,' Pansy reminded her. 'You said you would tell me on the train.'

'Oh, that fruit – yes, of course.' Laying her book in her lap, lifting her head in the lovely hat wreathed in flowers, Nonna began at the beginning, 'While you were still on the beach yesterday, Mrs Chubb came out into the garden and said there was something she wanted to tell me –' Nonna paused to wave away a fly.

'What was it?' Pansy prompted eagerly.

'She said how much she misses their family now they are

all grown-up and married and have left home, and although they come back with their children to stay sometimes, it isn't the same as having a child permanently in the house. She told me that she, and Chubb too, have taken a fancy to Leah and want her to live with them.'

'*Live?*' said Pansy. 'Always?'

'Yes, always,' Nonna smiled happily. 'The Chubbs are prepared to adopt her, if they are allowed to, and I don't think the Board of Governors or anyone else is likely to try to stop them. This is what my letter was about last night, darling. I was writing to tell the Pussies, and I suggested that Leah should return to the farm while everything is being arranged. Leah knows nothing about all this yet, of course, but I have no doubt that she will be back with the Chubbs in a day or two to stay for ever.'

'She'll have to double back pretty quickly if she's going to tickle the porker again.' Raising her eyes from her book, Atalanta blinked through her spectacles. 'They're going to turn him into pork any minute now.'

Pansy, who had been sitting staring at Nonna, smiled – a smile that broadened slowly into an enormous grin. 'Oh, Nonna, how absolutely *splendiferous*!'

If you have enjoyed this book and would like to know about others which we publish, why not join the Puffin Club? You will receive the club magazine, *Puffin Post,* four times a year and a smart badge and membership book. You will also be able to enter all the competitions. For details of cost and an application form, send a stamped addressed envelope to:

The Puffin Club Dept. A
Penguin Books Limited
Bath Road
Harmondsworth
Middlesex